CORRUPTION

Matthew Rudoy

authorHOUSE®

AuthorHouse™
1663 Liberty Drive
Bloomington, IN 47403
www.authorhouse.com
Phone: 1-800-839-8640

First published by AuthorHouse   06/01/2011

ISBN: 978-1-4567-5943-8 (sc)
ISBN: 978-1-4567-5945-2 (hc)
ISBN: 978-1-4567-5944-5 (e)

Library of Congress Control Number: 2011905013

Printed in the United States of America

For my grandfather, Irving Popkin, who taught me to love life.

ACKNOWLEDGEMENTS

I want to thank the following people for their help and support:

Jake Berntsen
Bradley Kavo
Morgan Riffle
Beth Rudoy
Debbie Rudoy
Paul Rudoy

CHAPTER 1

Ben Waxston sat behind the wheel of a stolen minivan, beads of sweat forming on his forehead. His hands shook as he veered the car sharply to the left. He ignored the shouts of protest from the four men sitting behind him and increased his foot pressure on the gas pedal. Anxiety overwhelmed him; his breathing came out in shallow rasps, his heart pounded against his chest. The daunting task he had been assigned to lead seemed more reckless than ever. This plan had been in the works for two months. Now that it was execution time, he was a nervous wreck.

"Slow down, Ben."

Ben cocked his head to the right, toward the passenger seat. A small edge of confidence soothed his apprehension as he glanced at his wife, Jessica. She was a slender, middle-aged woman with caramel colored hair tied back in a ponytail and a clear facial complexion. She normally wore dresses and skirts, but tonight her attire consisted of a black sweatshirt and jeans. Ben initially felt a much needed burst of confidence when he glimpsed his wife, heard her speak in that soft, calming voice she had, and saw that small smile upon those lips he had kissed so many times. As he eased his foot slightly off the gas pedal, his confidence was replaced by increased anxiety.

She should not be here, thought Ben sourly.

Originally, the group had been comprised of Ben and four other men. However, Jessica had wormed her way in the day before the mission was launched. She convinced Grassemer that it was her duty. All those years that she spent caring for her son had prevented her from being part of any mission. Grassemer granted her permission, claiming he was glad that another member would be added to the operation.

1

Grassemer.

The very thought of him angered Ben, the man who Ben still blamed for his best friend's death. Ben could not help but think that a decision made by Grassemer could yet again lead to the death of a loved one.

"Destination about a mile ahead," barked one of the men sitting behind Ben. Squinting into the distance, Ben also spotted their destination. The United States military base was not shrouded by the darkness of the night; it was visible from the two enormous lighted guard towers that lay at the edge of the base. Ben steered to the left, letting the car glide off the road. He then pressed down on the brake pedal, causing the minivan to come to an abrupt halt behind a clump of bushes. Unbuckling his seat belt, Ben turned around to face his four men.

"All right, this is it," said Ben, attempting to steady his voice. "We've been planning this assassination for two months. Everyone's worked too long and hard for anything to get screwed up tonight. We've all gone over this plan a hundred times. You all know your roles in this madness. Make sure all your machine guns are fully loaded; we don't want to corner our target with unloaded weapons. We'll all walk toward our destination as quietly as possible. Grab all the needed supplies. Try to make as little noise as possible on your way up and on your way down. Strap your machine gun around your neck or over your shoulder so your hands can be free. I'll go first."

Ben paused. "I have one more thing to say before we depart: only kill the soldiers if necessary. We are here for the sake of one man and him alone. Remember it is the Secretary of Defense, Dick Wilkinson we're after, not the soldiers. Am I understood?"

"Yes, sir!" replied the four men in unison.

Satisfied by the men's response, Ben turned toward his wife, determined to dissuade her. "Look, Jessica. I really want you to stay here," said Ben firmly.

"I can't let you do this alone, Ben. You need help; you and four others is not enough. Don't think that I don't understand the importance of this mission and what it means for the future. I've been with you since the very beginning. I've also experienced the hardships and sacrifices. I deserve this chance to help."

Ben sighed. Jessica always won their arguments; it had been that way since their high school days. Had he really expected to dissuade her when she had practically begged Grassemer to accompany him?

"Fine, I get your point. Just be careful, okay?"

"Of course," replied Jessica as she leaned over and pecked her husband on the cheek.

Five minutes later, Ben and Jessica were heading toward the military base with their four companions. Soon after, they reached the edge of the base, where a ten foot high chain link fence stood. Ben gazed at the guard towers which were illuminated by bright light, revealing the guards inside. Hardly believing their luck, Ben saw through the clear glass windows on both towers that the guards were slumped over in their chairs, fast asleep.

A few days ago, Ben had sent an anonymous package to the base, containing a box of chocolates spiked with sleep medicine. The chances of these two particular guards being on duty and eating the chocolates seemed too good to be true. Yet Ben cast aside his suspicions, and slung his machine gun over his shoulder as he beckoned one of the four men, Eddie, toward the fence.

Eddie was a brawny man, who was nearly seven feet tall. He had broad shoulders and bulging muscles. Eddie was a recent recruit to the cause Ben was part of, yet his value of membership would be tested in this instance.

"Ready?" asked Ben tentatively.

"Yes," growled Eddie in his deep voice.

Ben hoisted himself onto Eddie's shoulders and extended his arms toward the top of the fence. Eddie placed his meaty hands around Ben's ankles, ensuring that he would not topple to the ground. Ben grunted as he extended his arms as far as possible, his hands curling around the top of the fence.

"Let go," hissed Ben.

Ben heaved himself onto the top of the fence as Eddie relinquished his tight grip. Closing his eyes, Ben swung his legs onto the other side, and jumped. Ben opened his eyes as his feet made contact with the cement ground. The jump had been sudden, but he appeared to have safely landed. He turned around and gave a thumbs up to his comrades. The same procedure was performed for the three other men. Worried that she might injure herself after she jumped, Ben decided to catch his wife on her fall. Eddie, being the only one not yet inside the base, jumped as high as he could, managed to get a firm grasp on the fence, and jumped down like the others. As Eddie landed to the ground with a dull thud, Ben peered up at the guard towers, satisfied to discover that the guards were still asleep.

Now that they had breached the base, it was time to act. The visiting chambers where Dick Wilkinson resided lay fortunately close to the edge of the base. Hopefully it would be a quick job and the five companions would be driving away in their stolen minivan soon enough.

As Ben began running toward Dick's chambers, he caught a bright glint of light through his peripheral vision. Whirling around, Ben caught sight of Eddie, bathed in a glowing, stark white light. Bemused by this sudden turn of events, Eddie turned toward the direction of the light. Seconds after Eddie turned around, he emanated a brief, screeching cry as he toppled onto the ground, blood oozing from his forehead. Squinting, Ben spotted the place where the bullet pierced Eddie's brow. It took several seconds for Ben's brain to process what had just transpired, and then the truth dawned on him. But it was too late; Jessica was already running toward the bright light that illuminated Eddie's limp body, her grief overpowering her logic.

"Jessica, no!"

As Jessica entered the spotlight, bending over Eddie's body, two more gunshots were fired. Jessica's neck snapped backwards as she collapsed on top of Eddie's corpse.

Horrified, Ben turned his gaze away from the blood that was pouring out of his wife's neck, knowing there was no chance of saving her. All he could do was run toward the Secretary of Defense's chambers. Escape was now impossible. Death inside this base was inevitable. The only question was whether Ben would eliminate Dick Wilkinson before his life ended. Out of the corner of his eyes, he could see his three fellow men being gunned down as the bright, white light cascaded down upon them.

Forget them. You have a job to do, thought Ben.

Suddenly, Ben was roughly pushed to the ground by an unseen figure behind him. The right side of his face slammed against the cement ground as he fell. He raised a hand to his face in a vain attempt to forestall the bleeding. As he did so, he tried to heave himself back onto his feet, but he was yet again shoved to the ground. Ben stared up at his attacker, a tall and skinny man, muscular, with a pencil thin mustache.

The hunter had become the hunted.

Dick Wilkinson smirked as he stared down at his foe. He leaned over and muttered, "Remarkable, isn't it, how quickly one's role can change?"

Ben frantically reached for his machine gun which lay a few feet away, but it was to no avail. Dick plucked Ben off the ground by his shirt collar and punched Ben directly on the nose, causing blood to spurt out of it. Dick tightened his grip around Ben's neck. "Your wife is dead, her corpse will soon rot, and all because of you, Ben. You caused her to die." Ben tried to kick Dick in the stomach in an attempt to escape, but Dick countered his thinking by kicking Ben's stomach repeatedly. "You idiot," snarled Dick. "We knew you were coming. My Master always knows."

A soldier walked by Dick and tugged Ben out of the Secretary of Defense's arms. The soldier pinned Ben against the ground, while another soldier pointed a gun at his head. Dick watched the progression of events with deep satisfaction, a sneer etched across his face as he dug his hand into his pockets. He withdrew a long syringe and bent over Ben, chuckling.

"Five people died, including your wife, because of your decision to come here. But you need not go the same way. My Master has given me orders to spare your life for a worthwhile cause."

A humorless laugh escaped Dick's lips as he raised the syringe above his head and jabbed it into Ben's neck.

Chapter 2

Many miles away from the military base, a mother rapped her fist against a door in an attempt to wake her son.

"Five minutes, just give me five more minutes," moaned Jack Clark.

"Get up, Jack," called his mother, firmly, but not unkindly from behind the door.

Jack groaned as he slowly pulled off his bedcovers while his aching body begged to climb back into the soft bed. As he yawned, his hands brushed over the rough, bumpy texture of his face which was dotted with multiple bright red pimples, some filled with gooey pus.

Jack glanced in the mirror while he pulled his XXXL plain white t-shirt over his head, momentarily glancing at his flabby stomach. He didn't know if his physique resembled anyone in his family. Jack had no knowledge of any existing family members other than his mother. The only deceased family member she ever mentioned was his father, who had died when Jack was only a year old. She had never revealed the circumstances. His mother, Susan Clark owned a unique candy shop a few blocks away. The shop was unique because it was an independent store, rather than part of a chain. She had a difficult time trying to keep it open, but she somehow managed. She would often come home late at night, after Jack had fallen asleep, encumbered as she was by the responsibilities of owning and running an independent store. Having the privilege of being the son of the owner, Jack could take as many sweets as he wanted, free of charge.

As Jack caught scent of sizzling bacon, he quickly bounded downstairs. "Morning, Mom," said Jack, announcing his arrival into the kitchen. Susan

Clark brushed her jet black hair out of her eyes at the sound of her son's voice. She was a short woman of medium weight. Her face was dotted with a few pimples, but was nothing compared to the face of her son.

"Morning, Jack. The bacon will be ready soon. Did you sleep well?"

Jack nodded and placed a hand over his mouth as he stifled a loud yawn. He sat down at the breakfast table, and gazed around the kitchen. Shortly after doing so, Susan sat down, handed him a plate of bacon, and they gnawed on the crispy strips of meat.

"Anything of note happening at the store today?" asked Jack through a mouthful of bacon.

"As a matter of fact, something of note *is* happening today," said Susan after taking a long gulp of orange juice. "The CEO of Brownson's, as you know, has been trying to get us out of business and build another Brownson's. He keeps saying that independently owned businesses are the past; they all need to be eradicated. But business is booming. People can't resist stopping in for a box of chocolate truffles or chocolate matzah." She paused while draining her glass of orange juice. "The Brownson's CEO is sending one of his assistants to discuss the possibility of shutting down the business and turning it into a Brownson's. I think they're going to offer a considerable amount of money to me and all my employees for turning it into a Brownson's. But I'm going to forfeit the money, and keep the business going."

One of the aspects Jack loved about his mother was that she treated him as an equal and asked his opinions on matters that most considered Jack to be too young or unintelligent to comprehend.

"Your business is awesome, Mom. Definitely keep it going."

As Jack finished chewing his last strip of bacon, he glanced over at the two-handed clock on the wall, and saw that school started in ten minutes.

"Well, I guess I have to go to school now," murmured Jack. "I really hope that thing with the Brownson's guy goes well. Tell me about it when you get home from work, okay?"

"Absolutely," said Susan as she cleared the dishes off the table. She washed them off with a bright yellow rag, and placed them in the dishwasher. She paused, staring at the refrigerator, her mind drifting off into another world. Realizing what she was doing, Susan shook her head, returning to reality. She leaned forward, kissed her son's pimply cheek, and said, "Have a great day, Jack. I'll see you after I get home from work."

Jack watched his mother as she walked upstairs, grateful for the one person who cared for him, and wondering as he often did, if his father would have felt the same way.

Chapter 3

After brushing his teeth, Jack collected his heavy backpack from his bedroom, swung it over his shoulder, opened the front door, and headed toward school. It was a cool spring morning; a slight breeze blew against Jack's face. He walked down the cement sidewalks, past rows of modest, suburban homes, the local park, and the blossoming trees. Jack appreciated the scenes of spring, not because of the vibrantly colored leaves forming on trees or the balance of warm and cold weather, but because it meant summer was on its way. But it was not yet that glorious warm season of freedom, relaxation, and no school. Most kids accepted the reality that it was not yet summer, and they should just make the most of their time in school. For Jack, it meant nothing more than continuing to embrace his normal habits.

As he approached the school building from about a block away, he noticed that a man was standing in front of the steps that led to the entrance, staring at him. The man was a little over six feet tall. He had a gray beard that covered most of his face, but it did not grow off his chin. The man's head was balding, there were only a few wispy gray hairs left on his head. Throwing the black hood of his sweatshirt over his head, the man sprinted in the opposite direction of the school building before Jack reached the sidewalk.

By the time Jack reached homeroom, he concluded that it had been his imagination that the man with the black sweatshirt had been staring at him. It was more likely he had been checking to see if it was safe to cross the street.

Jack slumped into his homeroom seat, his eyelids feeling heavy, wishing that he was still sleeping. Meanwhile, the morning announcements ensued over the loudspeaker, which ended as usual with a piece of current news the principal classified as beneficial to the students' education.

"Last night it was confirmed that homosexuals inherently carry more than one contagious and fatal disease. Details on what these newfound diseases entail are still being gathered. Thank you for listening to the school morning announcements."

Conversation buzzed throughout the room as the announcements ended. "Homosexuals are so messed up," said a girl in front of Jack.

A boy sitting next to the girl smirked and said, "Good thing all those faggots are locked up now. Anyone who thinks that we should let them out of their confinement is crazy. All they do is spread their diseases. I bet you a bunch of stores will start selling those anti-gay signs and vaccinations for their nasty diseases again."

Several years ago, it was announced that scientific tests proved that homosexuals carry numerous fatal diseases that are contagious and cause sicknesses and deaths throughout the nation. Instantly, practically everyone ran out to the nearest drug store, ordering medicines to prevent the supposed diseases, and to the nearest clothing store for an anti-gay shirt. It was then declared that the diseases were so deadly and spreading at such a rapid pace that all homosexuals had to be placed into solitary confinement. The reporters on television claimed that this was not a discriminative move against homosexuals, but it was for the greater good of society, and for the overall safety of the American people.

One night at dinner, only a week after the reports were made, out of the blue, Jack's mother said, "These reports are, excuse my language, complete bullshit. It's ridiculous to even consider the notion that sexuality could be the defining factor in a deadly, contagious disease."

Even though his mother was the only one he ever heard deny that homosexuals carry infectious diseases, Jack believed her. She was the one person he trusted, the one person with whom he had a strong, positive human relationship. He valued her judgments above all others. Yet Jack knew she could be mistaken. There was a reason why the claims of a majority received more credibility than the claims of a minority.

But listening to the conversations around him, Jack was convinced that his peers were discussing a lie that they had been fed and obediently swallowed, that they were the fools, and not the other way around.

CHAPTER 4

After homeroom, Jack walked to his first class of the day, geometry. The teacher handed a pop quiz to his students as they entered the classroom. Jack blankly stared at the first problem on the quiz. Who cared what the measure of angle D was if the quadrilateral was 144 centimeters squared? Well, Jack figured that someone did care; otherwise geometry would not be a mandatory high school course. Jack understood the importance of geometry and its key role in architecture. However, this understanding did not cause him to like the subject anymore, nor did it diminish the idiocy he felt in the class every day.

After geometry, Jack headed off to his second period class, biology. When he entered the classroom, he spotted Ashley, a slender girl with fair skin, a smooth facial complexion, and short burgundy hair. She wore a black, waist high skirt, a smile forming upon her delicate lips as she greeted the handsome boy walking past her. Anxiously, Jack's heart raced as he strode toward Ashley in an attempt to socialize with her.

"Hey, Ashley, how's it going?" asked Jack in as kind and casual of a voice as he could muster.

The smile on Ashley's lips instantly evaporated at the sounds of Jack's words. She stiffly turned her head in Jack's direction, giving no response. Her eyes fell on the edge of Jack's nose, where an enormous pimple sat. Appalled that such an ugly boy would speak to her, Ashley walked away from Jack, and back toward her desk. She exhaled as the bell rang, signaling not only the start of class, but that Jack would have to return to his seat which was positioned in the opposite corner of the classroom.

Immediately after the bell rang, the biology teacher, Ms. Ferguson, a stout, elderly woman who wore spectacles and had curly gray hair stood up from her desk and barked, "Listen up everyone. Last week we studied mutualism, commensalism, and parasitism which are the three categories of symbiotic relationships. Judging by the quizzes you took last Friday, it appears that the majority of you understand these concepts. A few of you don't seem to have comprehended anything I taught you last week."

Ms. Ferguson's gaze lingered on Jack for a few seconds. It came as no surprise to him; he had paid almost no attention last week, and was forced to guess for every question on the quiz. He had expected to do poorly, but he did not care that much; he was mostly apathetic when it came to academics.

"For those of you who struggled, you're going to have to catch up on your own because we're moving on. Today, you're going to learn how symbiotic relationships affect evolution."

Uninterested as usual by her lecturing, Jack zoned out and turned his thoughts to the juicy, tender filet mignon he had had for dinner the previous night. He reminisced on the tangy flavor of the steak for the remainder of the class. When the bell rang, Jack squinted at the chalkboard and saw a good deal of scribbled notes he had failed to copy down.

After biology, Jack had history. Like his other classes, he had spent most of the year slacking off.

"Good morning, everyone," said the teacher, Mr. Jefferson. There was a dull reply from the students. "Now most of you may not realize this, but your final is coming up in a month." Several loud groans swept throughout the classroom. "Don't worry, I'm passing out the study guide right now. Besides, you've already learned most of what's going to be on the final. Both World Wars, the Industrial Revolution, the Spanish-American War, stuff like that you've already been tested on."

Jack pushed the study guide to the corner of his desk immediately after it was handed to him. He'd look at it another time.

Yeah right.

"Before I talk more about the final, I want to talk about a current event involving President Jones. Does anyone know what President Jones has been doing lately?"

"He's been chilling in the White House," replied a boy sitting behind Jack.

"Good guess, but wrong. Actually, Jones isn't in the U.S. right now. He's in the Middle East, trying to conduct peace talks between Israel and other Middle Eastern nations. Here's a video about it."

Jack glanced at the projector in front of the chalkboard and saw the

President of the United States, Brandon Jones shaking hands with several Middle Eastern leaders. Jones was tall, slim, had a comely, clean-shaven face, and a head full of slick black hair.

He was known for possessing a calm, yet powerful demeanor. Even while he discussed serious issues, even those that impacted life and death, he never became irritated or angry. Reporters would continuously pester him with the question, "What does it feel like to be President of the United States and not be married?"

Jones would always grin and respond by saying in his silky voice, "When a man has a family, it must be his top priority. His family must come before his job, his social life, his interests, anything. If I had a family to look after, they would be my number one priority. However, I am President of the United States, and I must always be focused on my job, whether I like it or not. My love and main concerns are currently to my country, which I have been blessed to rule."

Jack leaned back in his chair, choosing not to pay attention to the video, instead focusing on what he would buy for lunch. When it came time for lunch, he sat by himself at a table in the corner of the cafeteria, savoring each bite of his food. At home and restaurants, Jack ate much faster. But at school, he had learned to eat his food slowly. This made his eating experiences more satisfactory, was his one guaranteed source of enjoyment at school, and it ate up the entire lunch period. With no one to talk to, he felt there was nothing else to do but eat. Earlier in the school year, Jack had sat at other lunch tables, hovering on the edge of the table, nearly sliding off the bench. Although no one refused to let Jack sit with them, no one ever talked to him, normally ignoring his presence entirely. Whenever Jack tried to engage in conversation, his recipients either did not respond or gave him uninterested, bland responses before turning back to their friends. Feeling that it was fruitless to be uncomfortable and not talking with anyone, Jack decided it was best to sit alone. On the rare occasions he finished eating before the period ended, he would entertain himself by staring at Ashley who sat several tables away, surrounded by her giggling friends, their faces coated with makeup. Sometimes they talked so loud that Jack would catch snatches of their conversations which were centered on the latest gossip, the cutest boys, the most effective hair shampoos, and new fashion trends.

Jack spent the rest of the school day doodling in his notebook, letting his mind wander, and not paying attention in any of his classes. That was, until eighth period gym. Gym was by far the worst part of the day because

Jack was forced to participate. To make matters worse, Trent Owens was in Jack's gym class. Trent was tall, muscular, popular, the star of the baseball and football teams, and the meanest human being Jack had ever met. Trent enjoyed harassing Jack. No one ever stood up for Jack; everyone was too smitten with Trent's athletic abilities. But Trent's admirers were not limited to just students. The gym teacher, Ms. Kurbik, absolutely adored Trent. She could be seen at each of his games, cheering for him in the stands, later recounting his incredible performances, from his diving catch in the ninth inning of a baseball game, to the football game where he sacked the opposing quarterback on three straight plays. She admired Trent to such an extent that she did not oppose, and sometimes even subtly encouraged his belittlement toward Jack.

The class started as usual with Ms. Kurbik instructing them to stretch. For Jack, this consisted of nothing more than a few series of arm circles. This would be a simple enough task, if not for Trent's attempts to irritate Jack. Trent walked over to Jack, wearing a fitted black t-shirt which exposed his burly arms. Yelling loud enough so other students could hear, he shouted, "How's it going today, Fatty? You were probably upset with the burgers they served today at lunch. You're a fat ass, so you need, like, two triple-decker burgers."

Jack's face burned with embarrassment as the class exploded into laughter at Trent's cruel comment. Trent's remarks were never humorous, but they always seemed to amuse others, if only artificially.

"C'mon, aren't you going to answer me you fat piece of shit? Or are you more retarded than I think you are?"

Jack glared at Trent, wanting nothing more than to hurt him, make him pay for all the cruel things he had said throughout the school year. But Jack knew better. Ms. Kurbik and Trent would twist the story, and their versions would be believed. The majority of people would listen to a teacher and student athlete before they listened to a chubby kid failing geometry.

Ms. Kurbik walked in between students as they stretched, her eyes fixating on one person at a time, as if she was examining them. Jack guessed she was in her late twenties. She had short blonde hair and a wiry physique. Like every other day, she wore a sweat suit; the colors differed depending on the day. Being a Friday, the sweat suit was blue.

"Get stretching, Jack, or you're getting a zero today," growled Ms. Kurbik. She then turned to Trent and gave an approving nod.

Several minutes later, Ms. Kurbik blew here whistle and beckoned

16

everyone to gather around her. "All right class," bellowed Ms. Kurbik at an unnecessarily loud volume, "today we will be playing baseball. Trent will be one captain and Jack will be the other."

Ms. Kurbik always picked Trent and Jack as captains. She ensured that Trent had all the best athletes, and Jack had the worst. As usual, she took some of the more athletic kids that Jack selected and put them on Trent's team. She claimed she did this to make the teams fairer, but everyone knew she was just helping Trent's team win, another tactic to embellish Trent's superiority and Jack's inferiority.

Jack walked into the outfield, hoping that he would not have to move much during the game. However, this plan failed immediately seeing that Trent was up first to bat. On the first pitch, he hit the ball and it sailed into the woods, giving his team an early 1-0 lead.

"Go get the ball, Jack," screamed Ms. Kurbik, "you're captain!"

Sighing dejectedly, Jack sprinted off into the forest. He hoped he would be able to find the ball. If he didn't, Ms. Kurbik was most likely to give him an after school detention.

When Jack reached the forest, he noticed a set of footprints that appeared to belong to a human. Curious, Jack decided to follow the footprints, although it would probably lead to nothing significant. The footprints continued for a while until they stopped at the base of a large oak tree.

Two creatures stood ten yards away from him. Their bodies were in the shape of a human's, yet they were plastered in a thick, dark green slime. Assuming that the slime was a natural part of their bodies, they were naked except for the gray loincloths tied around their waists. A ringlet of yellow leaves hung off the chin of one of the creatures. They each held long metal rods, with sharp spikes protruding out of the sides.

After staring at Jack for several seconds, they turned to one another and spoke in a strange, gurgling language, exposing their pointed yellow teeth behind emerald green lips. Then they nodded and charged at the human standing before them, their spiked rods held aloft.

Jack's legs felt like lead; they refused to move. As the two creatures drew closer, it dawned on him that he was going to die because Ms. Kurbik made him chase a stupid baseball.

Just as they were about to impale their spiked rods into Jack, the same man that had been staring at Jack earlier that morning jumped out from behind a tree and began to fight the two creatures with a large sword, the silver blade gleaming in the sunlight. The man screamed, "Run, Jack!"

Not wondering how the man knew his name, Jack sprinted away from the horrific scene as fast as his stubby legs would carry him.

Jack emerged from the forest, panting, his pimply face streaked with sweat. As he looked around, Jack noticed that the whole class was gone, with the exception of Ms. Kurbik who sat in the dugout reading a magazine. He had been in the forest longer than he realized. Thinking that maybe she would not notice him, Jack began tiptoeing up to the track when Ms. Kurbik yelled, "Jack Clark, come here this instance!" Filled with dread, Jack turned around and walked over to the dugout. "Mr. Clark, class ended four minutes ago! Your classmates sat around patiently, waiting for you to retrieve the ball. However, we waited a long time as you should realize. Your laziness prevented us from having a productive class today. I'm giving you after school detentions for the next week as your punishment. You will be cleaning the men's and women's locker rooms. Never waste my time again. Am I understood?"

Jack nodded bitterly, figuring that it was no use telling Ms. Kurbik about what had happened in the woods. He trudged back up to the school building, terrified and bewildered by the horrifyingly fresh memory of the slimy creatures who had nearly killed him, and the mysterious man who had saved his life.

Chapter 5

"I'm sorry, Jack, but it's the way things have to be."

Jack sat at the kitchen table, his arms crossed. His mom had discovered that she had to go out of town for at least two weeks of meetings and negotiations if she wanted to keep her store.

"I really wish I could stay, dear, but if I don't go my store will be turned into one of the thousands of Brownson's out there, and I will be unemployed."

"Yeah, but the Brownson's people would give us a ton of money, so that wouldn't be a problem. Besides, I'm sure you can find another job."

"Jack, I don't want lots of money, because to live happily a person does not need tons of money. I love my shop, and oh, I'd be bored to death while you were at school if I lost my business." She stood up from her chair, went to the sink, filled up a glass of water, and returned to the kitchen table. She sipped her water for a moment before she resumed speaking. "By the way, I hired you a new tutor today."

"Mom, I told you, I don't need a tutor."

"Honey, you're not doing well in school. I agreed that I wouldn't hire anymore tutors if you worked hard. But you haven't kept your part of the bargain."

"Sorry, I'll work harder in the future."

"That's what you told me last time."

Jack threw up his hands in frustration. "School isn't your responsibility, Mom. If I don't want to work hard, then I'll face the consequences."

"But there's no need for you to face any consequences. You're a bright boy, Jack. All you need is to give effort. I think this new tutor is going to

19

motivate you. He stopped by when I was at work, and dropped off some reading he wants you to do before your first session tomorrow."

"But tomorrow's a Saturday!" protested Jack.

"You only have about a month left in the school year. At this point, every day counts. He'll come at eight o'clock tomorrow morning. Please be cooperative and obey him; he knows what he's doing. And make sure you do the reading before he comes, I left it on your bed."

Jack glared at his mother, his arms folded.

"I know you're unhappy about all this, but it's necessary. Please try to understand, okay?"

Begrudgingly, Jack muttered, "Yeah I understand."

He trudged up to his bedroom, his mind focused on the incident with the slimy creatures in the forest. He had considered telling his mom about it, but his disappointment about her leaving and the hiring of a new tutor drove the thought from his mind. Truthfully, he did not want the money Brownson's was offering. Jack wanted his mom to keep her store open. He had only argued with her because he did not want her to leave. Who would he talk to for the next two weeks (if it was only going to be that long)? As for the tutor, he found it annoying, a waste of time and money. It was worse than school, at least in school he could zone out. With a tutor, he couldn't space out with it being a one-on-one situation. That was one good thing about detentions. Although the work assigned was tedious, it didn't require much brainpower.

While scrubbing the filthy men's and women's locker rooms, Jack tried to convince himself that the slimy creatures in the forest had been figments of his imagination. There was, however, a major flaw with this rationale. He had seen the man with the gray beard and black sweatshirt twice, and he was convinced that he had not imagined the same man twice in the same day. The best plan of action was to simply keep his mouth shut and hope over time he would forget it ever happened. Jack suspected that blabbing about the occurrence would result in a visit to a psychiatrist who would declare him mentally insane or plagued by hallucinations. Too often, people were scared to recognize the truth. In their minds, it was better to lie and live under the illusion of a safer world.

As Jack entered his bedroom, he spotted a black notebook with a frayed cover propped up against his pillow. Jack was positive he'd never seen the notebook before, it definitely wasn't his. He stared at it for a few moments and then picked it up. The first few pages were crammed with words, but the rest of the notebook appeared blank. Then he realized it was the reading the tutor had dropped off. Not wanting to think about his mother's departure, the new tutor, or the incident in the forest, Jack began preparing for the one activity that always made him feel better: sleep.

Exhausted, Jack turned off the lights, pulled the bedcovers snugly up against his chest, and closed his eyes.

Before he fell asleep, Jack's thoughts wandered back to the bizarre incident earlier that day. Those long metal rods embedded with spikes that the strange creatures had been carrying flashed before his eyes. He could feel the pain, as if he was *now* being struck by those menacing weapons.

Once enveloped in a deep sleep, Jack found himself within a dream where he watched a woman walk up humongous steps made of white marble. Wherever the dream was, it seemed to be the dead of night; the sky was dark with the exception of the moon and the stars. The woman had a slender body, with long black hair billowing in the nighttime wind. Her face was somewhat tan. It was also flawless; there was not a single blemish upon it. She had pale blue eyes which were darting back and forth as if she expected someone to attack her. The steps, Jack realized, were leading to the Lincoln Memorial in Washington D.C. He had never been there, but he was able to identify it through pictures he had seen on television and in history books. Lincoln sat on his perch, his intimidating stare locked intently on the approaching woman's face, smooth as marble, just like his.

When the woman reached the base of the Lincoln Memorial, she gently set her black backpack down on the marble floor. Lying beside the base of the Memorial was a letter that Jack had not spotted at first; the white envelope blended in with the white marble floor. After reading the letter, the woman stuck it in her pocket. As she did so, a deep rattling noise echoed in the Lincoln Memorial. Three tall, hooded figures ascended the stairs, holding long swords that had such sharp edges that Jack believed they could chop off Lincoln's chiseled head in one swipe. The hooded figures were communicating to one another in monotone voices, enabling Jack to only be able to make out a few words. The woman, who saw the hooded figures long before Jack, climbed the steps and hid behind one of Lincoln's giant legs.

One of the figures started to move into the direction where the woman was. The figure was only feet away from her when…

"Jack, it's time to get up."

Enraged that he did not know what happened to the woman in his dream, Jack picked up his pillow, and hurled it at his door. He could remember every detail, even the most minor aspects of the dream: the color of the woman's eyes, her every expression, the black hoods of the strange figures.

Accepting that there was nothing he could do about it, he got dressed. When Jack went to the kitchen for breakfast, he saw that his mom was pacing nervously across the small kitchen. "You okay, Mom?" asked Jack with concern in his voice. Jack's anger at not knowing the fate of the woman in his dream vanished as he saw his mom looking more nervous than he had ever seen her before.

"I hope so, Jack. I'm just worried about how these meetings will go."

"You'll be fine, Mom. The meetings will go well," assured Jack. She nodded and then came forward and hugged Jack.

"I'll miss you very much. Make sure you bring in the mail and take out the trash every Monday. There's food in the fridge that will last you a few days and I left money on the counter so you can go out to eat. Lock the door behind you whenever you leave the house. Don't ever be hesitant to call me. I won't answer if I'm in a meeting, but I promise I'll call you back." She kissed him on the cheek and walked to the door, swung it open, and was gone.

CHAPTER 6

After eating breakfast and changing into a fresh pair of jeans and another plain white t-shirt, Jack decided to read the black notebook in his room. He had nothing better to do; maybe he could make a good impression on his new tutor by doing the assignments. He flopped down on his bed, and began to read the notebook, hoping it would be more exciting than the reading assigned at school.

The purpose of this journal is to record my daily observations and developments with the project. This journal is for me only, so if you are reading this, I dearly hope you are a fellow scientist building on the project and not an idiot who happened to stumble upon my records. In the unlikely event that my journal has fallen into the wrong hands, my logs are ambiguous enough that only someone familiar with the project will understand my observations and analysis. If the project succeeds as I envision, our world will be forever enhanced, we will take a major step forward in evolution, and we will attain an understanding of other species that was once thought to be unfathomable. I have tried to explain to my employers that this project will inevitably go far beyond politics. Sadly, they only view the project as a solution to fix a politically unstable world. I have only agreed to undertake this project because of what it means for science. Of course, they don't know that. They also fail to realize the complexity of the project. In fact, they're only giving me two weeks before it is freed. They haven't even revealed the first location where the project will be released. I have a hunch that it will be in the Middle East. But what am I doing, guessing the actions of politicians? I should be getting on with the creating process which I will hopefully be done with when I next write in this journal.

Day 1: Genetic transfers completed. Project is officially a living organism. Movements appear steady, crawling and flying is adequate (although this may not be the case when it leaves the glass tank and enters a natural environment). As expected, the MW I injected in the project and me is allowing us to communicate through telepathy. It appears intelligent, although currently it can only communicate through images which come from the inserted memory. I could read its mind, but the only time it sent images directly to me, it was associated with feeding off my body. I suppose I should be thankful for its innate desires, but I couldn't help but be frightened. Perhaps I rushed into this without thinking of potential consequences. What if in the end it does more harm than help? No, I'll make sure that won't be the case. I am determined to have this project better our lives on multiple levels.

Day 2: The resources inside the tank are already dwindling. I fear that I may need to restock the tank as early as Day 4. The problem is that I don't know if I can place more resources in the tank without the project escaping. This potential problem only adds to the mountain of frustration I am dealing with. Despite my forceful telepathic communication with both images and words, it refuses to learn. It is only interested in sustenance and mating. I tried to explain that the mating desire is futile because it can only mate with one of its kind, and it is the first to exist. Better luck tomorrow, I guess.

Day 3: Today was far more productive. The project actually responded to instruction and seems to easily comprehend information. MW is having exactly the kind of effect it should have on the project's brain. I taught the project about the alphabet, how to form words, and their meanings. It is incredible how quickly it processed the information. It now knows the entire alphabet, the spellings and meanings of a thousand words, and how to form sentences with these words. Our telepathic conversations can now be conducted through images and words. I see the images in my mind, but I hear the words in my head.

Day 4: Even though my employers would be disgusted by my lesson today, I felt compelled to explain the difference between good and evil and right and wrong. I'm sure they think morality will only hinder its ability to manipulate politicians, but I am convinced that this new species will be ethical. Through telepathic images, I conveyed the first four chapters of Genesis. I did not reveal the correlation between MW and the story of Adam and Eve in the Garden of Eden, such a revelation would be unnecessary to the task at hand. Besides, Chazerin, Wilema, and Grassemer would never forgive me. Exposing that piece of knowledge was never part of the bargain.

Day 5: More spellings and definitions of words taught today in addition to explaining the meanings behind the images from the inserted memory. The project now understands the words spoken within the inserted memory. I also tried to explain some basics of our world and different species. Obviously, most of the images within the inserted memory deal with humans so it already has a mediocre understanding of human beings (already far better than any other non-human creature). I spent several hours explaining much of what I thought the project should know about humans. Now that it has a decent understanding concerning the world, different species (humans in particular), and it knows the first four chapters of Genesis, I presented scenarios where knowledge of morality and facts needed to be used to arrive at a logical conclusion. It did well enough, although several times it was distracted by the tantalizing prospect of feeding on the bodies involved in the scenarios. It still views humans primarily as a food source, but not as much as it did on the first two days.

Day 6: If this project is going to fix our politically unstable world, it needs to know the history behind the instability. I expressed the human conflict and suffering of three major events in history that have shaped our lives. There is so much I would like to tell the project, but there is limited time. I considered starting with the Roman Empire, but I decided to instead begin with the Crusades. The Crusades is one of the best examples in history of beliefs and desires leading to chaos and bloodshed. My employers and I hope that by unleashing this project, we will prevent anything like that from happening in our lifetimes, and hopefully for eternity. I spent half the day giving information on the Crusades, and the other half on both World Wars. Now it has the knowledge to prevent these horrors from reoccurring.

Day 7: Breakthrough? I can't be sure, but it might be. For the first time, the project initiated a conversation. It wanted to know the purpose of my lessons. I explained as simply as I could what my employers want it to do, but also what I want it to achieve outside of politics. It was displeased by my response, especially by the expectations of my employers. Not only that, but it has a cynical perception of humans. It blatantly told me through strong words and images that humans seem to be the root of evil in the world. Most disturbing is that it explicitly told me that as a human, I am part of the evil entity that has corrupted the world. I'm happy that it initiated conversation, but worried by its reaction. Perhaps its cynicism is associated with the meager resources left in the tank. I suppose I'll have to think of some way to place more resources in the tank without letting the project escape.

Jack closed up the notebook after reading the last entry. He stared at the cover, vaguely wondering where it came from and who wrote it. It didn't seem like something that would help him do better in school. Although the notebook mentioned historical events such as both World Wars and the Crusades, and alluded to politics, and the Middle East, it didn't seem like reading for history. It focused on science more than anything else, and yet Jack doubted it would raise his grade in Ms. Ferguson's class. He had not understood most of the journal, and he suspected the unknown scientist would be pleased to know that ambiguity had successfully been retained throughout the observations and analysis. There were, however, a few facts that stuck in his mind. Most notable was that there were no records of the second week of the experiment. The project was clearly a living organism, but Jack could think of no organism that had the potential to do as much as the scientist predicted. For a moment, Jack considered presenting the journal to Ms. Ferguson and asking for her opinion. He chuckled, imagining her bewilderment at his first question of the year.

Unless she wrote the journal.

It was a possibility. And yet, Jack couldn't imagine his crotchety teacher creating a living organism that would forever change the world. She never expressed any opinion on politics. Maybe this was why. Then again, what reason did she have to discuss politics in a biology class? If Ms. Ferguson did write the journal, why had his new tutor assigned it to Jack? Maybe...

Maybe Ms. Ferguson was his new tutor.

Jack cringed at the idea of the grumpy old woman droning on about symbiotic relationships inside his home. Home was the one place where school couldn't interfere with his life. Apart from the homework that he only did occasionally, home was his one safe haven from school. No Ms. Kurbik or Ms. Ferguson, no Trent, just Jack and his mom.

This is stupid, Mom knows I dislike Ms. Ferguson; she would never hire her, thought Jack.

The doorbell rang. He glanced at the clock beside his bed. Sure enough, it was eight o'clock. Jack picked up the journal and walked downstairs, dearly hoping that Ms. Ferguson had not just rang the doorbell. Sighing, he opened the door to reveal his new tutor. Jack's body began to relax as he took in the sight of the figure standing in the doorway.

It was not Ms. Ferguson.

But it was someone Jack recognized. Jack's body stiffened at the sight of the tall figure, the black hood concealing his face, and the sword belted at his side.

CHAPTER 7

"Good morning, Jack. May I come in?"

Jack stared at the figure in the doorway, too shocked to respond.

"I'm your new tutor. May I come in?"

My new tutor has a sword, thought Jack dazedly, glancing at the black hilt. The blade was tucked inside a black sheath. However, it was not the sword that startled him, but the fact that the man standing before him was the same person who stared at Jack the prior morning, and then saved him from the slimy creatures in the forest. This meant only one thing: the incident in the forest had not been a hallucination. This man was real, and he had saved Jack's life.

"Uh, hi," said Jack, giving an awkward wave. Jack waited, but the man did not move or speak. Then he realized he had not answered the man's initial question. "Oh yeah, you can come in."

"Thank you," murmured the man as he crossed the threshold. As Jack closed the door, the man threw back the hood of his black sweatshirt, revealing his gray beard and balding head. He took in his surroundings, gazing around the house, and then refocused his eyes on Jack. "You seemed startled by my appearance. Did your mother not tell you I was coming?"

"She told me a new tutor was coming, but not you."

"What makes you think I'm not your tutor?"

"Because of what happened in the forest yesterday and because you have a sword," said Jack, gesturing at the man's waist.

"Didn't you realize that was your first lesson yesterday in the forest?" asked the man as if Jack had missed an obvious question on a test.

"You're telling me that nearly getting killed by those...whatever those things were was a lesson?" asked Jack incredulously.

"It wasn't a planned lesson; it just happened. It actually turned out to be a productive learning experience. You now understand the dangers of Treegonts."

"Sir, I have no idea what you're talking about."

"Of course you don't. But I'm going to help you understand. Soon enough you'll understand what transpired in the forest, the journal I gave you to read, the identity of your father, the circumstances of his death, and the truth behind President Jones."

Out of everything the man with the gray beard mentioned, there was one specific item that caught Jack's attention: his father. When he was younger, Jack pestered his mother with questions about him. Who was he? What did he look like? Was he nice? How did he die? Susan never told Jack anything more than that he died when Jack was a year old. He was a good man. That was it. The only time she was ever stern, the only time she refused to answer questions. Jack didn't even know his father's name. There were no pictures in the house. For many years, Jack clung to the hope that his father was not dead, that he would show up one day and would do all the things with Jack that a father and son should do. Eventually, Jack gave up on this distant hope and resigned himself to the fact that he was fatherless. But now, Jack was being told that he would learn the identity of his father and the circumstances of his death. Sure, he was curious about the journal and what happened in the forest, but that curiosity was pale in comparison with his desire to learn the truth about the man he'd wanted to know as long as he could remember.

"I definitely want to understand all that," said Jack. "Let's start as soon as possible. We can go into the kitchen, that's where I worked with my other tutors."

"I'm thrilled by your eagerness to learn, but first you need to know that we're not staying here. I'm going to tutor you on the road."

"Wait a minute. Slow down. You're talking about all this confusing stuff, but I still don't know who you are. What's this talk about tutoring me on the road? I'm not trying to be offensive, but you don't seem like the teacher type. How do you know as much as you claim to know, why do you know my name, why do you know who my father was and how he died, and why on earth do you have a sword?" Jack panted as the questions tumbled from his mouth. He'd managed to harbor his suspicions, but he couldn't help himself anymore.

The man grinned at Jack, seeming untroubled by the bombardment of questions. "You're not as apathetic as you appeared to be in your classes yesterday. You're definitely the man for the job. By the way, I apologize for not introducing myself earlier. My name is Grassemer."

Jack felt as if he had seen or heard the name recently, but he couldn't recall the context.

"How I know as much as I claim to know, particularly my relationship to your father, will be revealed soon enough. You'll soon understand why I have a sword and why I used it against the Treegonts in the forest yesterday. I'll tell you everything when we're on the road, with me driving."

"You're kidding me."

"Didn't your mother tell you to be cooperative and obey your new tutor?"

"Yes, but—"

"Your mother's instructions were clear. There's nothing left for you here, Jack. You won't regret coming with me. Destiny is calling you. Now listen to me carefully. We've lingered here too long; we have to leave as soon as possible. If there are any items that you find essential to your survival or you cannot bear to part with, gather them immediately. Bring the journal."

"But I don't—"

"Quickly!" said the man called Grassemer in an urgent voice.

Jack scampered upstairs, trying to think of a way to escape his current situation. It didn't make sense; his mother said she hired a tutor to help him with school, not someone who planned to tell the truth behind events Susan Clark most likely was unaware of. But there was nowhere to turn now. Besides, this Grassemer did show up exactly when his mom said the tutor would and he knew much of what she told Jack. Jack glanced about his bedroom, looking for a possession to bring along with him. There was nothing. He had clothes on his back, memories in his mind, and the other facets of his identity stored within places no one could touch. It felt incomplete, leaving his home with nothing but a notebook that was not his.

Just as he turned to leave his bedroom, an idea hit him. Then doubts began to creep in, telling him the plan would not work. But he had to try. Jack dashed down to the kitchen, thankful to see that it was deserted. He snatched the portable phone off the charger, and dialed his mother's cell phone number.

Ring. Ring. Ring. Ring.

Please pick up, thought Jack desperately.

Ring. Ring. Ring. Ring.

I have to know if this is what you wanted.

Ring. Ring. Ring. Ring.

Her answering machine came on, and Jack silently urged it to hurry up so he could leave a message. Then he heard footsteps entering the kitchen. The beep sounded in the telephone, and Jack made his decision. "Hi, Mom, I was just wondering what this tutor is supposed to work on with me, so just try to call back as soon as you can. Thanks." Jack hung up the phone, but it was too late.

"Who were you calling?" Grassemer eyed Jack suspiciously.

"Nobody."

"All right, then let's go."

Jack gazed around his home, attempting to drink in every aspect of it, hoping that he would one day return. As he reached the door, Grassemer threw the black hood over his head. "Follow me quickly and quietly," he murmured. Jack locked the door to his house and followed Grassemer down the street until he stopped in front of a blue sedan.

"Get inside." Jack did as he was told, opening the door and buckling himself into the front seat. Grassemer unbelted the black sheath from his side, and tossed it into the backseat as if it was a commonplace item. Then, he turned on the car, revved the engine, and with that, they were speeding out of the suburban neighborhood that was Jack's home.

CHAPTER 8

For the first twenty minutes of their drive, not a single word was spoken. Thoughts raced through Jack's head, the most frightening thought being that he had just been kidnapped. What he had envisioned as a boring tutoring session had turned into... turned into what?

As the car pulled into the Fort Pitt Tunnels which lead to the city of Pittsburgh, Grassemer broke the silence.

"What did you think of that journal?" said Grassemer, nodding at the frayed notebook clutched in Jack's hands.

Jack glanced out the window, through the faint darkness inside the tunnel, not knowing how to respond. He didn't trust this man, but he had yet to harm Jack. He even saved Jack's life the previous day. It seemed there was no harm by replying to the question. "It was interesting, I guess. But it didn't make much sense."

"You may not know what the project is, but surely you can gather enough facts to make an educational guess." The cars in front of the blue sedan halted, creating a minor traffic jam inside the tunnel.

Jack thought back on the journal, trying to recall what facts stuck out to him. "Well, the project was a living organism, the first of its kind. The scientist writing the journal thought the project would change science, politics, basically everything. I can't think of any organism that could alter our world so drastically, but I suppose anything's possible."

"Theoretically, anything is possible," said Grassemer.

"So you're saying that the project was only a theory, that the scientist's observations were what he would expect to happen?"

"No, that's not what I meant. Those logs are exactly how Roger

Pucknee perceived his creation. The project is as real today as it was when the journal was written."

"Look, I don't really care what that journal was about. I want to know about my father. That's why I'm here, not because of all the other stuff you said you'd tell me."

"You have to understand the journal before I tell you about your father. Listen to me, learn from my lessons. Ask questions, and I will reveal more about your father than you ever imagined."

Grassemer paused. "Before I tell you what the project is, you need to understand that the employers mentioned in the journal were a group of politicians who believed the world was on the brink of a third World War. They were panicking over rumors of nuclear warfare. If such events were to occur, and enough countries launched their nuclear weapons, there could be an apocalyptic outcome. In their desperation, these politicians turned to a prominent group of scientists who they thought might have the answer. The only one with any ideas was Roger Pucknee. He studied many fields of science, but nothing intrigued him more than the idea of intermixing species. The politicians wanted to persuade leaders around the world to refrain from launching their nuclear weapons, and to make decisions that would be beneficial at both an international and national level. Roger believed that leaders were stubborn; they couldn't be democratically convinced. In his mind, forceful manipulation was the only way to persuade politicians. He proposed an idea he had fantasized for years.

"His solution: create a parasite with human intelligence that manipulates leaders around the world. This parasite would take over the bodies of these harmful leaders, and force them to act as the American politicians dictate. The politicians immediately bought into Roger's idea. But as you know from reading his journal, Roger did not create this parasite just to satisfy a group of frightened politicians. He thought the parasite would enhance our world in many ways. Think about it: the ability to communicate with a non-human creature. The possibilities are endless, as Roger clearly conveyed.

"So, using his genius, Roger created this parasite with human intelligence. The exact process has never been discovered, although there are revealing tidbits in the journal. He used human intelligence and a human memory. I don't know if he took the body of a deceased parasite or if he formed his own. How he gave the parasite human intelligence and a human memory and a human life span, I don't know. Some complex genetic process only Roger could think of, no doubt. If everything had gone as Roger envisioned, the world would be a much better place. Sadly, like much else in history, the plan went awry. You saw in his last entry that the parasite saw humans as evil, that they destroyed the world. The parasite realized that the purpose of its existence was to be manipulated by Roger and those politicians. For a creature that's existence is based on manipulation, this does not sit well.

"You should know what happened next. The parasite escaped the tank and killed Roger when he tried to put more food inside. The parasite did not then aimlessly zoom about the world, feeding off random hosts. It was on a mission, a mission to destroy humanity, the species that tried to enslave it, the species that tarnished the world for their own sake with no consideration for other organisms. The first step in destroying humanity was to eradicate the most powerful group alive, the group that supplied Roger with MW, the substance that enhanced the parasite's brain and allowed communication even when the parasite was not inside a body. The group I'm referring to is known as the magicians."

Jack didn't think Grassemer's story could get any more ridiculous. It was so ludicrous to the point that he couldn't think of any logical questions to ask. From talks of a parasite with human intelligence to magicians. Utter nonsense.

The cars in front of the blue sedan began to move. Shortly after, the blue sedan was racing out of the tunnel, sunlight streaming through the windows. The sight of the city of Pittsburgh usually impressed Jack, from the towering buildings, to the historic bridges, the boats dotting the river, to the football and baseball stadiums, Heinz Field and PNC Park. Today, however, the sight was uninteresting compared to the confusion that clouded Jack's thoughts.

"You have not asked any questions thus far."

Jack noticed an edge of disappointment in Grassemer's voice.

"I haven't thought of anything yet," said Jack.

"What I'm telling you already has a profound impact on your life, you just don't realize it. I am siphoning the cloud of ignorance that obscures your perception of reality. I beg you to take advantage of this rare opportunity. Open your mind and ears. Erase your skepticism."

Jack was abashed by Grassemer's words, the implication that he was ungrateful. It was a strange feeling to have toward someone he hardly knew, someone who persuaded him to leave his home, if only temporarily. Yet this man Jack hardly knew had achieved what no teacher had ever done before. In that instant, Jack feared that his greatest weakness had been discovered: he could cave into others' will by feeling guilty.

Maybe this is what Mom meant when she said my new tutor would motivate me to learn, thought Jack.

"If you are going to understand the magicians and why the parasite thought they were the most powerful group of humans," continued Grassemer, "you need to know their history. Hundreds of years ago, an ancestor of mine stumbled upon a river. The water from this river had magical properties. When it mixes with one's blood it gives them special powers which became known as magic. In the journal, MW is an acronym for magical water. Someone who has MW mixed with their blood can summon anything that is truly natural, such as water, rocks, mud, tree bark, etc. For something to be truly natural and able to be summoned by magicians, it must be untainted by human touch or interference. In short, it needs to retain its purity to be summoned.

"The magicians can summon any pure nature made object, no matter how far away it is. However, the farther away it is, the longer it will take to come. They channel their magic through a desired part of the body known as the portal. The nature made thing which they summoned, will shoot out of the designated part of the body. A person will not feel any sensation in the spot where their magic derives from; in fact they will feel no pain whatsoever.

"My ancestor gave this magical water to a selected group who he felt deserved such powers. They dubbed themselves as the magicians, who would live normal lives, but surreptitiously help others around them with their newfound abilities."

"How?" asked Jack, glad to have finally come up with a question, even though it only consisted of one word.

"Anonymity. Never revealing our identities or purpose. We gave food to the starving, supplied natural resources to the government when needed, built shelters for the homeless, and lived out our own lives."

"Why don't I or most others know about the magicians? If they played such a major role in shaping our society and were always helping others, shouldn't we know about them?"

Grassemer chuckled. "The magicians can be found all throughout history; you just don't know it. Many of us fought for the United States in both World Wars. Soldiers, nurses, pilots, you name it. We were concerned with defending our nation, protecting our loved ones, and fulfilling our duties as magicians. You see, most of us led relatively normal lives. We were doctors, lawyers, policemen, soldiers, artists, politicians, athletes, almost any job you can think of. I suspect there were some criminals as well; I'm not naïve enough to think we were all outstanding citizens.

"Anyway, magicians were told to use their powers wisely, mainly to help those in need. Some used magic with their jobs; some only used it for charitable purposes. As long as we kept our abilities secret and did not abuse our powers, we could do whatever we wanted with our lives. The only other obligation was to come to the annual magicians' meeting in Wyoming."

"How many magicians exist today?"

"As far as I know, only five."

"Did there used to be more?"

"Absolutely. At one time, they were nearly five thousand of us."

"Five thousand! What happened to them?"

"You'll soon find out."

"Would I know any of the living magicians?"

"Yes. Two of them are in this car."

"We're magicians?"

The thought was the most ludicrous yet. Although, if magicians existed, Jack suspected he would peg Grassemer as one of them. His air of mystery, his sword, his intricate knowledge of the magicians. Actually, it made sense that Grassemer was a magician if his ancestor was the first one. Jack, on the other hand, felt about as magical as the grime floating in the Monongahela River.

"Yes, we're both magicians," said Grassemer calmly. "Now before you ask any more questions, I must continue."

"Wait, just a few minutes ago you were encouraging me to ask questions, and now you're telling me not to! No offense, but that's really hypocritical."

Grassemer did not seem the least bit offended. On the contrary, he was grinning. "Well done, Jack. You've already grasped the concept of arguably my most valuable lesson."

"What?"

"I contradicted myself by urging you to ask questions and then telling you to refrain from doing so. It was definitely hypocritical of me, but don't be surprised by my hypocrisy. All humans are hypocrites, ourselves included. The best we can do is try to avoid hypocrisy as much as we can and never allow it to trigger bigotry. Now, I'm going to continue on, but please ask questions. Disregard my earlier statement."

Grassemer paused as he veered the car onto the highway. The blue sedan whizzed past other cars, the only sound being the roaring of the engine until Grassemer resumed speaking. "So you see, the magicians thrived for several centuries, that is until my parents messed everything up." Grassemer spat on the steering wheel in disgust as he said this. "My parents, Chazerin and Wilema, led the magicians for three decades."

"That's where I saw your name!" exclaimed Jack as the revelation hit him. "In the journal, the scientist wrote something about you, Chazerin, and Wilema never forgiving him if he revealed something."

Grassemer was silent for a moment. "Yes, Roger did mention me. But that is unimportant. Now let's get back to my parents. At first they were strong leaders, but sadly, like so many other leaders throughout history, they became accustomed to their power, and began to crave more. Like an addiction. They believed that the magicians were superior to everyone else, and the magicians should overthrow weaker beings. A magician by the name of Dick Wilkinson, who is now the Secretary of Defense, accidentally discovered my parents' schemes. He was furious after making this discovery, furious that my parents were going to tarnish the noble tradition of magicians, just for the sake of power.

"The parasite, meanwhile, was delighted to learn of my parents' plan and Dick's anger, the perfect weapons to spark a potentially fatal war for the magicians. The parasite found Dick, claiming it was the savior of mankind, that it would help Dick restore the intended and pure ways of the world. According to the parasite, the first step to purifying the world was to rebel against Chazerin and Wilema. However, Dick was unpopular, and knew he did not have the support; there were very few people who would back him in any revolutionary attempts. The parasite, which was quite cunning with the superior human intelligence it had been given, made a deal with Dick. It promised that it would get people to back Dick in a rebellion against my parents as long as Dick pledged himself to the parasite for eternity. Dick immediately agreed, blinded by ambition. Taking control of another magician's body, a man by the name of Wirston, the parasite began to gather followers for Dick. Not long after, civil war broke out between the magicians. One side was led by my parents; another was led by the parasite, Dick, and his only friends, Tom and Durog."

"Did you join Dick's side because you knew that your parents had become evil?" asked Jack.

"First off, my parents hadn't become evil; they became power-hungry, which is an entirely different concept. At the time, I had no idea of the parasite's existence. It was only later, when I eavesdropped on the parasite's host, Wirston, that I learned the truth. I actually wanted to join Dick's side; perhaps if I hadn't things wouldn't have gotten so out of hand. But they were my parents, and nothing is more important than family, despite their flaws.

"It was a bloody affair, slaughter and turmoil erupting across the hills and mountains of Wyoming. How cruel it was that such atrocities should taint the natural lands where we had once gathered as a peaceful community. The magicians, once a group dedicated to bettering the world, were now blinded by hatred. Each side thought they were the righteous ones, salvaging the magician order, and the other side was comprised of greedy bastards.

"By the end of the war, the only surviving magicians were my parents, me, Dick, Tom, Durog, and the parasite's host, Wirston. It was unfair that the leaders, the ones who started the war survived while those who had been forced to pick sides were ruthlessly slain. The worst part was that the war accomplished nothing but the destruction of the magician order. All those poor souls died because a few morons wanted power. In the end, the only one with true power was the parasite.

"After the war, the parasite captured my parents and enslaved them. Using scientific information it garnered when communicating with Roger Pucknee, the parasite turned my parents into faithful servants."

"So your parents are still alive, but servants of the parasite?"

"Yes, they are referred to as Joinxs. They're alive, but they don't know anything except their Master's orders. The parasite has created one more Joinx since them, and I think it plans to create a whole army of those eternally dutiful monsters. Their minds are warped to the point that they don't know who they are anymore. They have no memories of life before they were Joinxs."

"What did you do after that, Grassemer? If the parasite, Dick, Tom, and Durog were all after you, where did you go?"

"I went to a small town in Texas where I figured I would be safe from my enemies, for a while at least. While I hid in this small town, my foes were busy at work. After much time spent scheming, they decided to infiltrate the world of politics. The parasite abandoned Wirston's body and disposed of him, partially because he was in poor health, but more so because the parasite wanted to take over the body of a man called Brandon Jones."

"Wait a minute," interjected Jack, "are you talking about the Brandon Jones who is our President?"

"The very same," replied Grassemer in an even tone.

"But then, that means…" Jack trailed off, too horrified to continue.

"Our President is not in control of his body or mind. He is manipulated by the same parasite that Roger Pucknee created, the same parasite that tore the magicians apart, the same creature that wants to destroy humanity."

CHAPTER 9

Jack sat in the passenger seat of the blue sedan as it sped down the highway, stunned by Grassemer's last assertion. Just when Jack was beginning to accept Grassemer's story, the whole thing seemed to lose its believability.

"It makes no sense," said Jack. "If this parasite you've been talking about is controlling President Jones, the United States would be launching nuclear weapons and starting wars all over the world, not conducting peace talks in the Middle East."

"Exactly. By appearing peaceful, no suspicion is drawn toward Jones. The extermination of humanity is happening under everyone's noses while they focus on the President. Also, some of the countries in the Middle East have nuclear weapons. The parasite wants to destroy humanity, and then inherit the purified earth, not lands ravished by nuclear devastation.

"Now back to what I was saying before, the parasite chose Jones because he was a well-liked politician with much influence in the political world even before his first term as a senator. He was rising quickly among politicians and most perfect of all, he planned to become President of the United States even before the parasite forced him into doing so. Meanwhile, Dick Wilkinson joined the military, and rose fast. He did this because he planned to become Secretary of Defense when Jones became President. The parasite also employed a species known as Treegonts."

"What are Treegonts?"

"They are the creatures that nearly killed you in the forest yesterday."

Spiked metal rods. Thick, dark green slime. The images flashed through Jack's mind, sending a chill down his spine.

"Treegonts were at one time nothing more than a myth," explained Grassemer. "There were stories of slimy, green creatures prowling through forests throughout the world, but they were nothing more than stories. It wasn't until they were recruited by the parasite that their existence was revealed to be factual. I don't know how Treegonts were created, or where they originally came from. I do know that they have a craving and passion for violence. This may not have always been the ways of their kind, but has been instilled in them by the parasite. Unfortunately, the parasite has employed the Treegonts to do much of its dirty work while it deals with the world of politics. Treegonts kill practically everyone they see, which somewhat satisfies their thirst for violence, unless the parasite commands them to refrain from producing bloodshed. Yesterday, the two Treegonts you encountered in the forest merely wanted to kill you for their own pleasure."

"And you saved me," said Jack, trying to put a note of gratitude in his voice.

Grassemer said nothing.

"So why don't most people know about Treegonts?" asked Jack, hoping for an answer to get Grassemer talking again.

"Because Treegonts do their job well," said Grassemer darkly.

Before Jack could fully process the implications of this statement, Grassemer was resuming his explanations.

"Along with Treegonts and the Joinxs, the parasite has another unknown group under its command. This group is an army of men that Tom and Durog assembled to commit violent deeds throughout the country.

"Meanwhile, the two Joinxs who really are my parents were sent to hunt me down and kill me while I continued to reside in that small town in Texas. At the time, I was the only magician alive who was not serving the parasite. And let me tell you, it is humiliating to know that your parents are hunting you, even if they have lost their grasp on reality.

"Eventually, the Joinxs found me, and I was forced to flee yet again. I became a hunted animal. The parasite, Dick, Tom, Durog, the Joinxs, Treegonts, and the army Tom and Durog had created were all after me. I knew that I would not survive long, so I retreated to a mountain in central Pennsylvania where I could be protected by the surrounding nature I could summon at a moment's notice if I was attacked. I aimlessly wandered about the mountain for weeks with no purpose in mind other than fleeing from my enemies.

"One day, I found an abandoned hotel nestled deep in the mountain. Inside the hotel were four teenagers. They were the first humans I had encountered since I found the mountain. At first I thought they were allied with the parasite. You see, my mindset had transformed into a constant state of paranoia. I discovered that they were accused of vandalizing and destroying part of their high school, which resulted in not only much destruction, but the death of a janitor. None of them committed the crime; the army of men assembled by Tom and Durog had done it. Knowing that they were innocent, they ran away to the mountain before they could be imprisoned, thinking like me, that no one would ever find them in such a location."

"So Tom and Durog's army damaged a high school and killed a janitor just for the heck of it?"

"The men have been brainwashed into thinking they are fighting for justice. Their perception is that each person they kill, each place they destroy, is an act of justice. I know it sounds crazy, but you don't know how influential Tom can be. They treat him like a god. He's not just powerful, he's clever. He always ensures there is conclusive evidence that frames someone entirely innocent as guilty for the crime he and his army commit. For instance, he specifically chose the four teenagers I found in the hotel to be the criminals.

"The sight of those kids was jolting at the time; it reminded me that I was not in a battle against the world. I rediscovered the importance of companionship as we stayed together in the abandoned hotel, all hiding from our enemies. I eventually brought myself to explain the true circumstances of their misfortunes, in addition to explaining much of what I am explaining to you now. Over time, I began to feel alive again, and I wanted to fight back against those who had wronged me, those four teenagers, and many others. Together, we began an organization called Walkrins, which still exists today."

"Who were the four teenagers?" asked Jack.

"One was Gregory Golish, who is now the leader of Walkrins. Another was Ben Waxston and his girlfriend who he later married, Jessica Chamberlain. The fourth member of the group was your father, Jason Clark."

Jack had forgotten about the real reason why he agreed to be tutored on the road. He smiled as heard his father's name, the name that he had not known until now.

"The five of us fixed up the hotel, transforming it into a rebel base," said Grassemer, recalling the memory with pleasure. "We began leaving the mountain to gather supplies, weapons, food, and allies, although at least one of us always stayed behind to guard the hotel. During one of his missions in a town nearby the mountain, your father stopped at a restaurant for a bite to eat. At that restaurant, he met your mother, and they fell in love. Their love for buffalo chicken wings was what first attracted them to one another. After dating for some time, your father revealed his true identity, and what he did for a living. Your mother was not appalled or frightened, but merely wanted to become a member of Walkrins. She did not care about Walkrins itself, she just wanted to be with your father and support him. Susan stayed with us for quite a while, that is until your father was murdered. As far as I know, no one from Walkrins has seen her since."

After a pause, Jack asked, "How did he die?"

Grassemer began to look uneasy after Jack asked this question. "Your father was on an important mission the night he was murdered. A spy committed to Walkrins had caught Brandon Jones on video talking about his plans, but really it was the parasite's plans. Your father was going to give this video to a national television station that was going to broadcast the video so the public would know the truth. If your father had succeeded, the parasite's host would never have been able to become President, and its many horrific schemes would have been ruined. But it was not your father's fault. Nobody knew of this plan other than me, and the other four founders of Walkrins. Jessica, Ben, and Golish would never have betrayed your father. I mean, they all admired him, and were good friends. But someone else knew, because your father was intercepted on his mission by Tom and Durog. Your father put up a valiant fight, but in the end, Tom killed him. Tom then blamed Jason's death on one of his men, so he would not have to go to prison. Durog and Tom destroyed the video, erasing any evidence of the parasite's plans."

Jack was silent for a moment, reflecting on the tragedy. "How do you know all of that if my father went on that mission alone?" asked Jack, suddenly suspicious.

"Several hours after your father had left," continued Grassemer, "it was clear to me that something was wrong, he should have returned. I followed the path he was supposed to have taken, and found Durog who was erasing evidence of what had transpired. I captured him, and brought him back to the hotel as my prisoner. I interrogated and questioned Durog for hours, and discovered lots of information. Much of what I have told you thus far concerning the parasite, I learned during that interrogation with Durog. Not long after the interrogation, Durog killed himself. I don't think he could handle the prospect of potentially facing his friends and Master that he betrayed. I offered to let him join Walkrins, but he declined. I knew Durog long before the magicians' civil war. He had been a friend of mine. It was yet another horrible time in my life. I lost Jason, my loyal friend, and Durog, who I hoped to redeem before it was too late.

"Every day I wish that I had gone on that mission instead of your father. In a way, his death is my fault; I was the one who suggested he go on that mission. I suggested him because I trusted him more than anyone else; I knew he would not let me down. It would have gone over well if we hadn't been betrayed." Grassemer paused. "I know that there is at least one filthy spy within the midst of Walkrins. Since then there have been numerous times that the enemy knew everything about our plans. Recently, Ben Waxston went on a mission with five other Walkrins' members, a mission to murder Dick Wilkinson. All the Walkrins' members were killed, except for Ben who was kidnapped and turned into the third Joinx. Had the mission succeeded, the parasite's most powerful and influential ally would be dead, and the parasite would have less control over the military without a Secretary of Defense who is on its plans. The point is that it's hard for Walkrins to plan anything when there's always a chance that the parasite's spy knows about the plan."

"Are you sure your spy who gave you the video didn't betray Walkrins?" asked Jack, determined to know the full truth about his father's demise.

"I've considered it as a possibility, but it can't be," said Grassemer confidently. "I never told our spy who was going to deliver it, or even when. No, it definitely was not him."

Jack waited for Grassemer to continue speaking. Two minutes of silence ensued, leading Jack to assume the explanations were finished, at least for the time being. He glanced out of his window and saw empty fields, farms, and forests. The blue sedan was alone on the road. It struck Jack how far away from home he was, and how long he'd been sitting in this car. Grassemer was certainly knowledgeable, but not in the way Jack expected his new tutor to be. What Jack had learned from his first session was interesting, but he didn't understand what it all meant. Why did he deserve such information?

"So what was the purpose of telling me all this?" asked Jack, turning his gaze away from the window.

For a second, Grassemer took his eyes off the road, and turned to Jack, wearing a solemn expression.

"I told you all that information because you possess rare abilities, rare abilities that will help you fulfill your destiny: slaying the parasite."

CHAPTER 10

Jack's head was spinning. Grassemer's words echoed in his mind, their implications and meaning.

"I think you've got the wrong person," began Jack slowly. "I hate to break it to you, but I have no abilities that could help destroy the parasite. I'm just a useless kid." Grassemer opened his mouth to speak, but Jack cut him off as he plowed on. "I'm slow, fat, and I have horrible reflexes. The only fight I've ever been in was one time when I got really mad at Trent. He gave me a black eye, and embarrassed me in front of the whole gym class. You call that heroic? And by the way, I'm one of the ugliest people on the face of the earth. No one whose face is covered in pimples and can't finish running the mile in gym class has that kind of destiny, even if destiny does exist. If I get my butt kicked by Trent, how am I supposed to defeat one of the most powerful creatures to ever live?"

"Do you have no self-respect?" said Grassemer, a note of disappointment in his voice. "Being negative is only weakening yourself and strengthening your enemy. A positive attitude can be as effective against an enemy as a sword or magic. In fact, a positive attitude can be one's greatest weapon that will never fail."

"Oh yeah," said Jack cynically, "how so?"

"All those years that I was being hunted and had to fight to survive each day, my positive attitude was better than any weapon. Every day I told myself that there was something better around the corner, and that my survival would help others. I never succumbed to my enemies; I continued to fight back, even when I was outnumbered one hundred to one. If I had been negative, I just would have given up, and I would not be sitting here today. Walkrins wouldn't exist if I hadn't been positive all those years. Do you understand?"

"I guess," muttered Jack. He hesitated. "That still doesn't explain what special abilities I have that will help me kill the parasite."

"Your special abilities come from the magical water within your body. Remember what I told you earlier: you're a magician."

This tidbit of information had slipped Jack's mind among the hoard of other facts thrown at him. It seemed unlikely. Then again, none of this was the least bit likely.

"Even if I am a magician, that doesn't explain why I'm the only one who can destroy the parasite. You said there are four other existing magicians other than me, including you. So, why aren't you or the others capable?"

There was a pause and then Grassemer replied, "This is not the appropriate time for me to divulge that information. However," he put up his finger as Jack tried to interrupt him, "I promise that I will tell you. Eventually, anyway."

Jack's stomach began to rumble, they had been on the road for nearly four hours, and Jack wanted lunch.

"Uh, Grassemer, are we going to be stopping for some lunch soon? I've usually eaten by this time at school, and well, I'm just really hungry." Jack had been so focused on what Grassemer had been telling him, that Jack had forgotten about eating, which was rare.

"We will be reaching our destination soon where we can hunt something for lunch."

"Did you say we will *hunt* our lunch, or did I just not hear you correctly? Now that I think about it, you haven't even told me where we're going!"

"I'm taking you to a cornfield which is about thirty miles south of the mountain where Walkrins resides. We will spend two weeks at this field during which time I will train you. I will teach you how to use your magical powers, to control them, and the basics of magic. Normally, I would spend much more than two weeks to train you, but a mere two weeks is pushing our already limited time. You need to go to Walkrins. The people need you. They need a symbol of hope, one who they can put faith in."

Jack snorted derisively. "Me, a symbol of hope! One who people can put faith in! Grassemer, like I said before, I'm just a useless kid."

"Your youth is an advantage if anything," said Grassemer. "Take my advice: stay positive. This is what's best for you. It's what your mother wanted."

"So she knew all this," said Jack, disappointed by his mother's concealment. "Why did she keep so much from me?"

"I don't know for sure, but I suspect she feared you would want to join Walkrins once you learned the truth. She wanted to keep you away from war and violence. But I was able to convince her that the time had come to comply with your duties, to do the right thing."

So she didn't think I could I handle the truth, thought Jack. Then another thought struck him, one far more disturbing.

"She's in danger."

"Who?"

"My mother. They've probably captured her already. Quick, turn around, we have to go—"

"Calm down, she's perfectly safe," said Grassemer in an assuring voice. "I sent members of Walkrins to protect her in case she is attacked. She should be able to carry on with her business meetings. Besides, I doubt the parasite would bother harming her. Our enemy has far more pressing matters to attend to."

This last assertion sounded just as convincing as the other facts Grassemer shared. Satisfied that his mother would be safe, Jack's thoughts wavered back to his hunger. "Is it possible to conjure food from magic?" asked Jack.

"Yes, but only certain kinds. As I told you earlier, anything completely natural can be summoned by magic. So you could summon an apple which grows naturally from an apple tree, or potatoes grown from the ground. But you cannot summon French fries, even though the key ingredient of potatoes is natural. You can only conjure food which is entirely natural and untainted by humans."

Thinking this over, Jack decided that magic would only be able to get him fruit and vegetables for the most part; the double cheeseburger and potato chips he had been hoping for would have to wait. "What about meat?" asked Jack.

"Animals cannot be summoned through magic, although, I wish they could. Being able to summon a rhinoceros during a battle would be quite effective. When we're in the cornfield, however, you can hunt any animals we see with your magical skills."

They continued to ride through the empty countryside for a while longer, Jack's thoughts wrapped around all Grassemer had told him and his rumbling stomach.

"Ah, here we are," murmured Grassemer. Jack peered out the window and saw the cornfield, abundant in stalks of corn, but nothing else. As Jack stepped out of the car, the first thing he noticed was the stifling heat, a nasty surprise after the cool air-conditioning in the blue sedan.

"Beautiful, isn't it?" sighed Grassemer, gazing around the cornfield.

"I guess," said Jack with a shrug, "if you really like corn."

Grassemer appeared not to hear Jack; his mind seemed to be a million miles away judging by his vague, dreamy expression. Jack looked around for trees where he could find shade, but all he could see were endless rows of corn stalks.

"I remember the last time I was here," murmured Grassemer.

"You've been here before?" asked Jack in surprise. He couldn't imagine why anyone would come to a cornfield more than once (unless they loved corn).

"Yes, I have. This is the only place where the beast is silent."

"Sorry?"

"Within each human being there is a monster, a monster which is tethered by a leash forged of a power too great for any of us to understand," explained Grassemer. "The monster rears its head every now and then, but it is not until it breaks the leash that a person is in trouble."

What the hell is he talking about? thought Jack.

"Cool, so what are we going to do for lunch?"

"Well," said Grassemer, stroking his gray beard, "we have several options. We could eat corn provided by these corn stalks. We could attempt to hunt our food, although that will be difficult, nothing worth eating usually comes through here. Or, I could begin your magical training by showing you how to summon natural foods through magic."

"Show me how to summon food through magic because the other ways are gonna take too long. We'd have to cook the corn because it's raw, that'd take a while, and it sounds like hunting is pointless."

"Very well, we will begin your training now." Grassemer cleared his throat and stated, "This magic does not involve spells or wands. In fact, you don't have to say anything to perform magic. A mute person could complete this magic, because no verbal activity is involved. It only deals with the mind. First you must choose what part of your body you would like your magic to emanate from. This area is known as the portal. Most choose the hand as their portal, but I do know of a few who have done their eyes, nose, and ears. I would suggest the left hand—"

"Sure, I'll do my left hand," said Jack impatiently. He was now semi-wishing he had gone with the corn, cooking it over a fire might not have taken as long as this. Magic was already far more complicated than Jack had anticipated, and he was sure that Grassemer was only sketching the surface of this new concept.

"Good choice," said Grassemer enthusiastically. "The hand is the easiest to use, especially during a battle. No matter where one chooses their magic to emit from, the person will not feel it, even if they are to summon scorching hot lava from a volcano, or a freezing cold block of ice. Now you must focus only on the spot of your hand from which you want your magic to derive from. You must focus on this for exactly sixty seconds. Do not let any other thoughts interrupt you in this time-frame. Are you ready? Do you know where on your left hand you would like your magic to come from?"

Jack nodded apprehensively. He knew this would be difficult while thoughts of greasy pizza and chocolate chip cookies with the gooey chocolate chips melted would continually cross his mind.

"Begin now," instructed Grassemer.

Jack's thoughts turn to the center of his palm. Every inch of flesh and skin and beads of sweat upon the center of his palm was the center of attention. Chocolate milkshakes and giant bowls of his favorite soup, lobster and crab bisque continued to swim across Jack's mind. He pushed these thoughts away, keeping his focus on the sweaty center of his palm. He continued to focus on the center of his palm for what seemed like an eternity, far more than sixty seconds, until finally...

"Time's up."

Jack breathed a sigh of relief; he had held his breath for most of the sixty seconds. All of his concentration and attention had been on the center of his palm.

"Good job, Jack. You showed that you have strength, perseverance, and a high mental capacity." Jack thought Grassemer was assuming too much. He did not feel he was at all strong nor had a high mental capacity.

"Now for performing the actual magic," began Grassemer. "It has similarities to what you just did. You have to concentrate on whatever you want to summon, but remember, it must be naturally made. Think about what you want to summon, to the point where you can practically see it before your eyes. You said you wanted to eat, so focus on some type of food. Put all your attention on this desired natural food, think about how much you want it, and stick out your hand, because that is where the food will come from."

Jack began to focus on an apple tree, with red, juicy apples hanging from the branches. He began to concentrate solely on the apples, he stuck out his palm and he waited for the apples to come. Jack felt nothing, but then he heard Grassemer saying, "Jack, stop, stop!" In alarm, Jack opened his eyes and stopped thinking about the apple tree. In astonishment, he saw that he had indeed summoned apples; about ten of them lay at Grassemer's feet.

"I didn't realize, I mean I—"

Jack could hardly talk due to a mix of hunger and his shock that he had produced actual magic. "I didn't feel anything so I thought I hadn't summoned any apples."

Grassemer chuckled. "I told you earlier that you wouldn't feel what you are summoning, no matter what it is. You did well for a first attempt. The next two weeks, I will teach you how to summon more difficult things, and more importantly how to control what you are summoning. Remember that you are actually summoning these natural things from real places. Somewhere, an apple tree has lost about ten apples that have never been tainted by humans."

"So can I eat these now? Are they edible?"

"Yes," said Grassemer, smiling, "eat them all if you want to." And with that, Jack began to gnaw at the apple closest to him, thinking that he had never tasted anything so wonderful in his life.

Chapter 11

Soon enough, Jack's days spent in the cornfield became routine through a training program Grassemer devised. Grassemer would wake Jack up at precisely eight o'clock in the morning each day. He would then have Jack do a series of strenuous stretches, followed by a ten minute jog. Jack had never liked exercise to begin with, and therefore found it sheer torture to stretch and jog each morning.

"Why do I have to do this?" panted Jack as he clutched his aching sides.

"Because you need to be in shape," said Grassemer calmly. "To fight and to utilize magic takes energy. You may have magical abilities, but your body still tires and functions as all human bodies do." Grassemer hesitated for a moment. "I don't want to sound rude here, but you really do need to lose some weight. Exercise is good for you, and I know you don't believe me now, but you'll be thankful you did this when you've lost weight. I don't care how a person looks, but in this case, it is unhealthy to be so heavy, and I want you to be as healthy as possible."

Jack had endured enough criticism at school, having to complete physical exercises he was not capable of, listening to lectures about how he should lose weight, not to mention how everyone, particularly Trent belittled him for being fat.

"So what do you want to do about my acne?" snapped Jack, who tried to sound angry in an attempt to mask the sadness and disappointment he felt at hearing Grassemer's comments. Jack had believed that Grassemer was one of the few people who didn't judge others by their looks, but by their traits, personalities, and choices.

"I told you, Jack, I don't care how a person looks. As far as I know, your acne isn't harming you, it just looks bad. But your weight is hazardous to your health. What a person is truly like is what matters. Too many people get married or date one another just because of physical attraction. But fifty years later when that person is wrinkly, their hair has turned gray, and they walk with a cane and a limp, they regret marrying for looks only. I believe that the body is merely a shell that carries a person's mind and soul. Some of us have nicer shells or bodies than others. The best people sometimes have a dreadfully ugly looking shell or body, but that should not have an effect on the person they truly are. The quality of one's shell is usually not synonymous with the quality of what lies inside." The corners of Grassemer's mouth twitched slightly, but he quickly covered it up with a solemn expression

"So you're not attracted to good looking people?" asked Jack, skeptical of Grassemer's odd belief.

"I was at a time, mostly when I was younger, but I have learned to look past what I see on the outside, and focus on the inside. I look at you as an equal, Jack, because of the person you are. I have not judged you as a person at all by your looks. Even though one's shell should not be a predominant factor when judging others, you must keep in mind that you need to keep your shell healthy. You cannot survive without your shell."

"So how do you judge people when you see them for the first time?"

"Well, initially the majority of my judgment is based on their shells because I have nothing else to base my judgment on. Once I get to know a person, their shell becomes a meaningless aspect in my opinions of them. Do you understand?"

Jack nodded. Even if he had not understood what Grassemer had been saying, he would not do anything other than nod. Jack figured that an argument with Grassemer would be futile. If Jack ignited an argument, Grassemer would only talk more about his peculiar theory and regardless of what he said, Jack was sure that Grassemer would still make him jog for ten minutes every morning.

After stretching and jogging, Grassemer would have Jack do something with magic in order to obtain the food for breakfast. Whether this was Jack summoning the food, or Jack trying to move the food toward him using magic, it had to apply magic for Jack to eat.

"You will work for every meal you eat in these next two weeks, always using magic," said Grassemer, who was cutting up strawberries that Jack had summoned.

Then, Jack would listen to Grassemer while he told Jack important details about Walkrins, magic, and the war they fought. This lasted until noon exactly, when they would break for lunch. Like breakfast, Jack had to work for his food. Jack was doing well with his magical abilities overall, except for control. When Grassemer was teaching him how to summon components of something natural (this time it happened to be lava from a volcano) Jack summoned too much lava, resulting in the disintegration of several corn stalks.

Grassemer continued to train Jack in his magical abilities until six o'clock, when, like breakfast and lunch, Jack had to work for his food. Jack summoned potatoes, thinking that they would be good, but he found that they were quite bland, not like the French fries and baked potatoes with melted cheese he was used to eating. Thinking about a way to give the potatoes more flavor, Jack summoned tomatoes thinking of ketchup on French fries. He squirted the tomato juice on several of the potatoes, but found that it tasted nothing like ketchup.

After this unsavory meal, Grassemer retrieved a football from the trunk of his car, and would throw it with Jack for an hour. Grassemer made Jack run complicated routes to catch the ball. Just understanding the routes was difficult enough, but Jack also had a tough time catching and throwing the ball. Once the ball slipped out of his fingers and went behind him when he tried to throw a pass to Grassemer.

"Why do we have to do this?" moaned Jack. "I'm never going to play football; it only makes me feel lousy about myself."

"It is important," said Grassemer while stowing the football back in the trunk, "because it is another form of productive exercise and it requires concentration. A key part of being a successful magician is concentration; you cannot let other thoughts infiltrate your mind. Even while you are fighting in a battle, and bullets are firing past your head, you must keep your concentration. Your magic will not work unless you focus on it clearly, but at the same time, you must pay attention to what is happening around you. In a football game, you must concentrate on not only running the route or throwing the ball at the right time, but also throwing a good pass, and managing to catch the ball while knowing how to overcome the defensive coverage. Do you understand?"

It was an odd way to teach concentration on multiple things at once, but Jack saw some logic to it. The exercise was certainly not the method Jack would use, but there was no doubt it was unique.

After their hour of football, Jack got his only true break of the day. He and Grassemer would either sit in between the corn stalks, or in the car. Usually Grassemer would lie between the corn stalks and gaze up at the stars with a dazed look on his face. Grassemer seemed to be in a completely different world, a world without war and no power-hungry parasite: a world of peace. Then his mentor would fall asleep while gazing up at the glistening stars. They were more visible than Jack had ever seen them due to the lack of electricity and other forms of manmade light. Jack would sleep in the backseat of the car, his face pressed against the black leather, thinking about what he had learned, and his mother, whom he missed dearly.

CHAPTER 12

Jack's training continued in this pattern: he continued to jog, learn and use magic, and sleep in the backseat of the blue sedan. Jack's dreams were blurred, and he could not remember them as usual. The dream he had had about the beautiful woman chased by the strange, hooded figures had almost been forgotten until the fifth day of his training.

After jogging, Grassemer as usual talked to Jack about Walkrins, the war, and magic. He asked Jack, "Have you had any dreams lately where you could remember everything about them when you woke up?" Jack raised his eyebrows in surprise, wondering if Grassemer was about to explain the dream he had had about the beautiful woman.

"As a matter of fact, I have," said Jack slowly. "I had a dream that was clearer than any I have ever had before. Every detail was razor sharp, I felt as if I was almost there. The most peculiar thing is that I could remember everything about the dream when I woke up in the morning."

Curious, Grassemer asked Jack, "Can you tell me about this dream?" So Jack told Grassemer everything he could remember about the dream, even the most insignificant details.

"Ah, this is interesting, quite interesting. The reason you were able to remember this dream so clearly is because of your magical abilities. Those with magical water within them have dreams of real events that are happening in the present. What you dream about has some connection, whether big or small, to your life."

"So that dream was actually happening? That woman was really at the Lincoln Memorial and being chased by those hooded figures?"

"Yes," said Grassemer, nodding. "The woman in your dream is a member of Walkrins. Her name is Sarah Setter. Around the same time I went to Pittsburgh to find you, she went to Washington D.C. The letter that she picked up was from a spy who is committed to Walkrins. Those hooded figures were the Joinxs. Two of the three you saw in your dream were my parents; the other one was Ben Waxston, who was turned into a Joinx after his failed attempt to murder Dick Wilkinson. The question is: did Sarah escape? You say the Joinxs were closing in on her?"

Jack nodded, suddenly feeling panicky. For some reason, he felt a strong connection to the woman, as if he had known her for all of his life.

"Well, we can only hope she escaped. She is quite resourceful, that's why Golish assigned her that mission."

"Why haven't I had any other dreams like that?"

"These dreams do not happen every night. You're still going to have normal dreams. You will only have the ones caused by the magical water within you on rare occasions. When you do have these dreams, take note of them, you have to remember they are real, and they will have some type of impact on your life. The bottom line is that they are far more than just dreams."

"I now understand *what* these dreams are, but I don't understand *why*. Why do magicians dream of the present and why can we recall our dreams so vividly?"

"No concrete answer has been formed as to why this occurs; many magicians have speculated on the logic behind our dreams. My theory on the matter is that magical water infuses the ability to attain nature within us, and therefore, our dreams reflect the time period of our lives that is most natural: the present. The past is tainted with illusions and the future is uncertain, whereas the present is pure and real. What we are able to summon through magic is pure and real, so the same happens within our dreams. I believe we are able to clearly remember every detail of our magical dreams because the present is easy to recollect, unlike the past or future which is the time period in which those without magical water dream in."

After this discussion, Jack began to continuously think of the woman from his dream. She had been so beautiful, so poised, and so brave. Sarah Setter was far more attractive than Jack's high school crush, Ashley. In fact, Jack began thinking that Sarah was the most gorgeous person to have ever lived. At these thoughts, Jack had to pinch his arm or smack himself in the face. He hardly knew anything about the woman, yet he felt as if he was in love with her, or at least he was infatuated. Any time when Jack was not practicing magic or listening to Grassemer, his thoughts went to his mother, the woman from his dream, and the difference between love and obsession. Unable to keep his thoughts to himself anymore, Jack asked Grassemer during the eighth night of their training, "Grassemer, have you ever been truly in love?"

Jack had been somewhat afraid to ask Grassemer this question. It was quite personal, and he asked Grassemer this question while he was looking at the stars, in his own little world. Chuckling to himself, Grassemer said, "Why so curious, Jack? What does it matter if I was ever in love?"

Slightly embarrassed, Jack said, "Well, uh, I don't know. I've just, uh, been thinking about love and that, that type of stuff lately."

"No one's ever asked me a question like that."

"Sorry," said Jack, whose face had turned red from embarrassment. "It was too personal of a question."

"No, no," said Grassemer patiently. "You are a good person, Jack. I know that you won't go around gossiping what I tell you, and truthfully you could use it. My goal in these two weeks is not only to teach you about magic, but about life as well. Many never know if they truly love someone or if they're just infatuated, especially if their relationship was not long-term. To truly love and to be obsessed with a person is entirely different. There was once a woman who I believe I loved, or maybe I was just besotted, who knows. I met her when I ran away to that little town in Texas after my parents were enslaved by the parasite. Most of the time I was there, I spent with her."

"What did she look like?" asked Jack, curious to know what type of woman would win Grassemer's heart.

"Give me a second to conjure up an image of her. Let's see. She was plump and short; I was more than a foot taller than her. She had curly black hair which she rarely combed. What I found most alluring was this thoughtful expression she'd get on her face. She'd gaze off into the distance, her face scrunched in concentration, her eyes narrowed as she paced back and forth, muttering under her breath." Grassemer sighed. "But it was not meant to be."

"Are you still with her? Are you married?" asked Jack, wondering why Grassemer had not mentioned this woman before.

"Unfortunately we never did get married. We were going to, but certain events prohibited us from doing so."

"What do you mean?"

Grassemer did not immediately respond. His eyes took on a far-off look, but it was not dreamy and vague like his expression upon arriving at the cornfield. Blistered by painful memories, Grassemer winced, the muscles tightening in his face. "I've said enough for now. Good night, Jack," said Grassemer, an edge of coldness in his voice. He turned away from Jack, throwing his sweatshirt hood over his head as he squirmed on the ground, attempting to place his body in a comfortable sleeping position.

Jack closed the car door, curling up on the backseat, a pang of guilt hammering away at him. He feared he had delved too deeply into Grassemer's personal life, asked questions he had no right to know. Not wanting to dwell on his guilt, Jack closed his eyes, allowing his mind to wander elsewhere. Before he knew it, he found himself thinking of his father. Grassemer had conveyed more information than Jack could comprehend, and yet Jack still knew precious little about this man called Jason Clark, the man who helped give birth to the pimply teenager lying in the backseat of the blue sedan parked beside a cornfield. There was so much more Jack wanted to know about him, but he felt apprehensive of asking questions after Grassemer's last reaction. But his thirst for information concerning his father was too great. He knew he would, no he *must* ask about him before the two weeks of training ended. Satisfied with this solution, Jack attempted to relax his mind, and fall asleep.

An hour later, Jack was still awake. His eyes skimmed the interior of the blue sedan, searching for something, anything that might help him fall asleep. The only object in the car was Roger Pucknee's journal. Jack felt he had a more than adequate grasp on the information contained within the journal, but he had nothing better to do, so he scooped it off the floor and began to reread.

For the most part, the journal made sense and fit with all the information Grassemer had revealed. However, there were a few sentences that did not seem to fit, that seemed almost out of place. And they most certainly did not correspond with anything Grassemer said.

I did not reveal the correlation between MW and the story of Adam and Eve in the Garden of Eden, such a revelation would be unnecessary to the task at hand. Besides, Chazerin, Wilema, and Grassemer would never forgive me. Exposing that piece of knowledge was never part of the bargain.

From what Jack could gather, Grassemer and his parents had made a bargain with Roger Pucknee. The bargain seemed to deal with magical water and knowledge concerning the beginning of Genesis. Striking a bargain with the creator of the parasite led Jack to only one conclusion: Grassemer had been responsible, if only partially, for the creation of the parasite. The thought was startling, but its likelihood was questionable. Jack couldn't see why Grassemer would want such a creature created. Knowing what little he did about his teacher, he found it hard to believe that Grassemer would buy into the idea that the parasite would fix a politically unstable world. As for the argument that the parasite would enhance the world of science, Jack suspected Grassemer would have an even more difficult time buying into that idea. Grassemer didn't seem like the type who would endorse a project where so much could go wrong, nor did he seem like someone who would place the world's future in the hands of one creature. All Jack could deduce from these sentences was that Grassemer was somewhat responsible for the creation of the parasite. Why he had been involved in the first place, Jack had no idea. Regardless of why Grassemer may have been involved in the first place, Jack had no doubt that he regretted his affiliation, and that he was now fully committed to destroying the parasite.

Jack closed up the journal and tossed it back onto the car floor. He couldn't help but feel slightly suspicious of Grassemer, but he still trusted him for the most part. In a way, Jack felt as if it almost didn't matter if Grassemer had played a role in creating the parasite. All that mattered was that he was now intent on destroying the creature and he had found the boy destined to complete the job. There was nothing to gain out of no longer trusting Grassemer. There was nowhere to go; he was stuck with his teacher in the cornfield. Besides, he couldn't be that bad. According to what Grassemer said, he had accomplished some remarkable feats throughout his lifetime. Most importantly, it appeared that Susan Clark had wanted Jack to learn from him. If she trusted him, that was good enough for Jack.

These thoughts continued to weigh on Jack, but he eventually fell asleep before what seemed like only minutes later, he was woken by Grassemer. Grassemer did not seem any different than usual. If Jack had irritated him through pestering him with questions the prior night, Grassemer did not show it. The day progressed with training as the other days had. The only difference was that after their football session, Grassemer began flipping through channels on the car radio.

"I want to know if our enemies are up to anything," explained Grassemer as he turned away from a broadcast of a baseball game. "Their doings usually end up in the news, even though the facts are often distorted."

Snippets of talk came from the radio, but Grassemer turned away only seconds after turning to each station.

"A bad traffic jam in—"

"Costs raised by one percent—"

"An irresistible sale at—"

"International relations at an all-time low for—"

"Would you say homosexuality is the biggest issue in America right now?" Grassemer did not turn away from this station. He let go of the controls and leaned back in his seat, letting the radio broadcaster's words fill the car.

"Homosexuality is the greatest danger Americans currently face, and therefore the biggest issue in our country right now," replied another voice. "Homosexuals carry some of the most infectious diseases ever known to mankind. As of right now, we know of no vaccine, no way to combat this threat."

"Do you have any reason to believe a vaccine will be found in the near future?"

"I'm afraid not. It's not just that we haven't found a solution to this problem, but we're not getting any help. Other nations refuse to accept the sad truth. We've been trying to tell them that denial will only make things worse, but they won't listen. This is the bottom line: solitary confinement is the only answer. Homosexuals are not bad people; they're just unfortunate to have been born with disease in them."

"What advice would you give to those who currently live in fear of homosexuality?"

"If you suspect anyone of being a homosexual, report them to the authorities immediately. If this country along with the rest of the world is to survive, we can't be exposed to them. Be a good American, defend your country. Let us maintain the land of the free and the home of the brave, where we will be free of infectious diseases."

Grassemer let out a low growl as he turned off the radio. "The grand plan is working," he muttered.

"What's the grand plan?" asked Jack, unsure of whether Grassemer was talking to himself or not.

"It is a plan that was created by the parasite," said Grassemer softly, turning his head toward Jack. "The plan is based on the parasite's claim that it will perfect the flaws of humanity."

"What do you mean, perfect the flaws of humanity?"

"The parasite doesn't really care about helping humanity; it's just a clever ploy to rally supporters and allies. The parasite promises to eliminate the flawed aspects of humanity such as our greed, vanity, wickedness, and any imperfection that hinders or threatens us. Truthfully, the parasite just wants to kill these people or enslave them, but the whole idea of perfecting humanity is a clever cover up, for human beings are constantly seeking perfection that they fail to realize does not exist. The first move of perfecting humanity's flaws was claiming that homosexuals carried fatal diseases, and they were therefore put into solitary confinement."

"That's horrible!" said Jack, disgusted by the lengths the parasite would go only so it could gain power.

"Yes, it is," said Grassemer, nodding gravely. "The worst part is that after they were imprisoned, most of them were killed. Most of the deaths were staged as accidents or relatives and friends were told that the prisoners committed suicide. Next it will be the mentally unstable who are said to be a hazard to our society because their addled brains can make them do things that could harm us. After they are taken care of, the list will continue to grow until all of humanity is either enslaved or killed. To be quite honest, the homosexuals were one of the best minorities the parasite could have targeted. Think about it: you can accuse anyone of being a homosexual because it is not part of their physical makeup. It has been more effective than if the parasite had targeted someone based on skin color or physical deformities."

"How was it pulled off?"

"The parasite left the body of Jones and controlled others, but it was mainly through bribery. Scientists were paid to forge convincing evidence that proved homosexuals carry deadly diseases. Then the bigwigs at major television stations were paid big money to report the startling new discovery, although it's not as if they wouldn't have reported it anyway. Once the media got hold of the false information, there was no stopping it. What's most clever is that the parasite ensured that the money was given anonymously. No one can testify where it all began."

"It's prejudiced," said Jack, who felt a mix of revulsion and fright at hearing the parasite's plan to eradicate the human race.

"You're right, Jack, it is prejudiced. Prejudices form from hatred. Hatred is all the parasite has ever known. From the moment it learned of the intentions of Roger Pucknee and the panicked politicians, it hated the fact that the purpose of its existence was to be manipulated. It wanted to be the one doing the manipulating. Full with such spite, the parasite formed a vendetta against its creator and the entire human race. Although the parasite has the lifespan of a human and prime human intelligence, it is not the most superior concerning emotional intelligence. The parasite does not realize the nature of the prejudices it is exploiting in order to gain power.

"You know, many members of Walkrins joined the organization because they have some relation to the group that will be marked as a hazard to society next by the parasite, or they understand that if the parasite's plan works, they will eventually be on that list, regardless of who they are. This is largely why I helped create Walkrins in the first place. I refuse to let hatred and prejudices be the causes that destroy the world. Furthermore, the human race should not be annihilated just because of the mistakes a scientist and my parents made many years ago."

Exhaustion coursed through Jack's body, for not only had night fallen, but the complex information Grassemer had just given him seemed to drain his energy. He looked into the front view mirror of the car just before he was about to go to sleep, and saw that his face was quite hairy.

Jack stroked the new stubs of black hair, feeling the new texture on his face. In a way, Jack liked his new look more. This new rugged appearance was more appropriate for what he was becoming. Jack also liked the fact that his facial hair would cover up some of the pimples on his face. Feeling good, Jack laid down in the backseat of the car and fell asleep.

CHAPTER 13

On the thirteenth night of Jack's training (which was also supposed to be the second to last night in the cornfield) Grassemer extracted a surprise from the trunk of his car.

"Beef jerky!" exclaimed Jack.

"Yes," said Grassemer, his expression transforming into a wide grin. "I was going to save this for the last night, but like you, I was craving meat."

Grassemer opened the package and tossed a piece to Jack. Normally, Jack wouldn't have liked beef jerky very much, but seeing as it was the first meat he had had in nearly two weeks, it was spicily delicious. Jack and Grassemer quickly and easily devoured the bag of beef jerky and then went to throw and catch football as usual after dinner.

Jack had improved tremendously with the football exercises. His passes were now usually spirals and they were on target, unlike the wobbly, off target passes he had thrown during the first few days. Also, Jack hardly ever dropped a pass anymore, he even caught a pass from Grassemer one-handed, and was running most of his routes correctly. After placing the football back in the trunk, Jack asked Grassemer something that had been weighing on his mind for quite a while. "What was my father like, Grassemer?"

"What do you know of him?"

"Not much," replied Jack. "Basically all I know is what you told me about him. Mom never talked about him much. I've been trying to remember any memory I may have had of him but I don't have any. I was only a year old when he was killed."

"I suppose it is only natural to be curious, and I did know Jason for quite some time," said Grassemer, his voice much quieter and less firm than usual. "Your father was an uncommonly kind man who always looked for the best in people. He was a generally positive, upbeat, and happy person who enjoyed telling all kinds of jokes, whether they were off color, corny, or funny. Jason was a true individual, who rarely jumped on the bandwagon, and almost always tried to do the right thing. In high school he had only two friends: Ben Waxston and Jessica Chamberlain, who later married. The high school he went to was full of druggies, alcoholics, lowlife scumbags, and even a few criminals. To be part of a group, or have many friends at this school, one would have to join these hoodlums. But your father never did, he always remained himself. After he and his two friends, as well as Gregory Golish were wrongly proven guilty for vandalizing their high school, they fled to the mountain where I met them and together we created Walkrins."

Grassemer began to examine his hands as if he did not want to look at Jack while speaking to him. "Like I said before, your father always looked for the best in people. For example, Golish was always negative, and a drug addict. No one seemed to want to give him a chance to redeem himself, including me. I will admit that I did not trust him. But your father insisted that Golish would help create Walkrins. I could never explain to Jason what foresight he had in that decision. Golish has become an excellent leader of Walkrins."

Grassemer opened his mouth as if he was about to say something else, but he merely closed his eyes and lied down in between the corn stalks. Jack wanted to hear more about his father, but it was obvious that Grassemer had said all he had wanted to, at least for the evening.

I wonder if Dad would be proud of me, thought Jack, wishing for what seemed like the millionth time that his father was still alive.

Shortly after lying down, Jack heard a car pulling up behind the blue sedan. Curious, Jack raised his head, and peered through the window. Two ragged looking men stepped out of a battered red truck, their hands curled around the holsters belted at their sides. As one of the men spotted Jack staring at him through the window, he withdrew a pistol from his holster, and began shooting at the window, which shattered only after the first few bullets were fired. Jack ducked and rolled onto the floor in sheer panic. The man who had shot at the window was now trying to climb through it in order to get to Jack.

Just as Jack thought his life was about to end, the car went into reverse, and spun around. A loud scream echoed across the road as the man trying to get into the car was thrown out of the window and onto the street. Jack glanced up and saw Grassemer sitting in the driver's seat, looking like a wild man with a ferocious expression on his face.

"Are you all right, Jack?" cried Grassemer over the roaring engine of the car.

"Yeah," said Jack, but he sure didn't feel all right. "What, what happened? Who were those men?"

"I would guess that those men work for Tom. I went to the cornfield with Tom many years ago. I guess he remembered and thought that might be where I was training you, so he sent two of his men to confirm if his suspicions were accurate. We're just lucky that Tom didn't show up."

"So what do we do now?" asked Jack shakily, trying not to sound as frightened as he truly felt.

"We head to the Walkrins' base. The two men are probably tailing us. Even if they aren't, they'll report back to Tom, and he will be after us."

Jack looked behind him, but saw no cars. "I don't see any cars; I don't think they're tailing us."

"All the same, we must get to Walkrins as soon as we can. Now, I need to make a phone call and then we need to have an important discussion." Grassemer kept one hand on the steering wheel and used his other hand to dial a number on his cell phone. For a moment there was silence, and then Grassemer was speaking in an urgent tone. "Our training location was discovered. We need to get to the base as soon as possible. Bring Ryan and as many gunmen as you can fit in the helicopter. Land at site B. Keep the priority of the mission in mind, just like we talked about. Do you understand?" An indistinguishable voice replied and then Grassemer hung up.

After a slight pause where Jack could hear the wind howling outside of the broken car window, Grassemer resumed speaking. "Jack, there are several essential matters I need to discuss with you now. You must give me your full, undivided attention. Tom and his men may catch up with us at any time. It is imperative that you listen carefully. Do you understand?"

"Yes, but—"

"No interruptions," said Grassemer sternly. Grassemer cleared his throat and resumed speaking. "You asked me on the journey to the cornfield why you have magical powers, and why you are the only one who can destroy the parasite. I was going to divulge this information during our last day of training, but unfortunately current events have changed my plans. The reason—" Grassemer stopped speaking as a car with bright headlights pulled up behind them. As it came closer, Jack saw it was a police car, but it simply sped past them.

"That was a close call," said Grassemer. "Anyway, back to what I was saying. To have magical powers you must have had at least one parent who was a magician or you must be injected with magical water. If one is given a certain amount, it will make all their blood magical, thus giving them special powers. Your mother and father weren't magicians, so—"

"I was injected with it?" interjected Jack.

"Please," said Grassemer, lifting a hand. "During the last night you spent at home, I snuck into your house, knocked you out, and injected you with the last magical water on earth." Jack remembered how he had felt a sharp pain in his arm that night, but he had thought that that had been attributed to thinking about the Treegonts' weapons.

Just as Jack was about to interrupt again, Grassemer continued speaking. "My ancestor took a great deal of MW when he discovered the magical river, but he did not take as much as most thought. One of the reasons that my parents wanted to take over the magicians was because they knew that there was hardly any MW left to give to new magicians who didn't have magical parents. The parasite and its allies stole all of the MW that was left, except for one bottle that my father gave me. I've been keeping it all these years, waiting to give it to the right person. I chose you, Jack, because you deserve it, and you will use your powers well. I watched you during the last day you spent at your high school, partially because I wanted to see if you were anything like your father or mother, but I also wanted to see if you were worthy of receiving the last magical water on earth. Your life has been full of misery with no friends and only your mother caring about you. All these years I realize that you have wished over and over again for somebody to come help you, somebody to be your friend. You wanted someone to help you live a happier life. Understanding this will enable you to help those around you who truly need help, which you will be able to do with your magical powers. I've given you a purpose in life, something we all need. Every kid wants to feel special. Now you have that opportunity.

"The other question you asked was how I knew you were the only one who can destroy the parasite. The truth is I have no proof whatsoever that you will or will not destroy the parasite. I don't believe in destiny. Everything doesn't happen for a reason, sometimes things just happen. I have made it public that you are the only one who can destroy the parasite for several reasons. The people of Walkrins are in complete disarray, we are weak in many aspects and Ben's ghastly fate and the deaths of his companions have done nothing to help this. The bottom line is that the people of Walkrins need something to believe in and to keep them going, day in and out. By telling them that Jack Clark, the son of Susan and Jason Clark, is the only one who can destroy the parasite, gives them hope and a reason to continue to fight in this war, where Walkrins is currently losing desperately. Also, it has created fear among our enemies. The parasite is now deathly afraid of you, it refuses to confront you because it is scared that you will destroy it. You are a symbol of hope for our allies, and the greatest threat to our enemies. Jack, you must never tell anyone what I have just told you. Do you understand?"

"So there's no prophecy, or anything at all that says that I'm the only one who can destroy the parasite? I mean, you have no proof at all?"

Grassemer shook his head. "I don't believe in destiny, fate, prophecies and all that other junk about what's supposed to happen in the future. Life just happens as it goes. The fact you have such strong-minded parents, and you have magical powers gives you somewhat of an edge, but other than that I have no evidence that you will destroy the parasite. In fact, I have no idea how to destroy it. I mean, even if you would kill its host, there's still the thing itself. When I captured Durog, he told me that he saw the parasite's true form once, and it was about the size of a fly. Incredible isn't it, the damage a thing the size of a fly has done?"

Jack stared out at the sky, tinted red by the setting sun. Despite almost two weeks worth of magical training and the fact he was in the best shape of his life, he felt just like the old, unconfident Jack that used to be bullied by Trent back at school. The pressure and weight of what people would expect from him when he got to the Walkrins' base was even worse. All these thoughts and emotions layered on top of one another, forming a pyramid, building to the point at the top where the despairing truth was perched.

I was betrayed.

"You lied to me," said Jack in a hurt voice.

"It was necessary," said Grassemer simply.

"Necessary? You call lying to me about my purpose in life, necessary?"

"Don't complain," said Grassmemer in a voice that suggested Jack was being foolish. "I've given you a purpose in life, it's just not predestined."

"I don't care that it's not my destiny, I just don't like that you lied!"

Grassemer gave a soft chuckle. "You're so noble, Jack. That's why I like you. In your heart, you believe that it's always better to tell the truth than to lie. But one day you'll realize, like me, that lying can be so much more...effective."

"Maybe small lies, or even just one, but not tons of lies!"

"What are you suggesting?"

"That you were involved in the creation of the parasite, that you and your parents were the employers, not a bunch of panicked politicians."

"I wasn't one of Roger's employers. That, I did not lie about. I won't deny that I contributed to the project. I knew Roger from college, and he knew of my real identity. He asked me for MW, thinking that it could enhance the intelligence and abilities of the parasite. I talked with my parents, and they agreed to comply with Roger's wishes. We didn't do it as a favor; we did it because we believed the parasite could help with our plans, plans that I originally told you only dealt with my parents. Truthfully, I was right in league with them. I was almost as power-hungry as they were. But the parasite backfired on us, just like it backfired on Roger and those frightened politicians. Even after a full-scale rebellion had begun, I insisted to my parents that we stay on course with our selfish schemes. It was my brother who was the one who defied our parents. He tried to tell both my parents and me that we were being fools. He told us that we would eventually lose our power, and we were going to learn that the hard way if we attempted to carry out our greedy plans. But we didn't listen to him; we were too blinded by our future visions of ultimate power. My brother didn't join either side during the magicians' war. He tried to remain neutral. One day, Dick Wilkinson had me cornered and defenseless. He was just about to kill me when my brother jumped in, sacrificing his life in order to save mine. After the death of my brother, I realized how horrible war truly is, and that one's beliefs become seconded when a loved one is in danger, as in the case of my brother. I named the organization that fights back against those that killed my brother in his name: Walkrins."

Jack let this information sink in before asking the other question on his mind. "What happened to the woman you loved?"

Grassemer gave an exasperated sigh. "Jack, I've told you enough as it is. What happened to her does not concern you."

"Yes it does. I need to know how you dealt with people close to you after the magicians' war. I deserve to know."

Grassemer hesitated. "I suppose you have a legitimate point. Around the time I was planning on getting married to the woman I believed I loved, I caught wind that the parasite had discovered the location of my safe haven. The Joinxs would soon arrive to kill me. So I fled. Alone."

"You abandoned the woman you loved?" asked Jack, now feeling more appalled than angry at Grassemer.

"I deserted both her and someone else who was close to us. The Joinxs found her and tortured her in attempt to extract information about me. She could offer none, I had never revealed my past to her, and I hadn't told her where I'd gone. Once the Joinxs realized she was of no further use, they killed her. My parents killed the woman who had almost been their daughter-in-law. I was selfish. I left her to an undeserved fate while I saved my own skin. Any love I may have had for her was usurped by narcissism."

Grassemer gave a resigned sigh. "Well, now you know the truth, Jack. I'm a murderer. I killed countless magicians during our civil war, magicians who had at one time been friends and peers. My supposed great love died because of my cowardice. I told myself she'll be a burden to carry; leave her to her own whims. Some lover I was."

Grassemer's head whipped around. "Don't become like me, Jack. Be better than me. Be better than all of us."

Grassemer refocused his eyes on the road, leaving Jack to his own thoughts.

So, Jack had been deceived. Grassemer had woven a fantastical destiny for him, and Jack had swallowed it as easily as everyone swallowed the lie about homosexuals. Who was Grassemer to give Jack a seemingly impossible task, a burden that no one had been able to fathom the means to accomplish? It was amazing to consider that so much fear and hope could be induced in so many by one lie. What would everyone expect? Did members of Walkrins think that Jack was going to confidently trot up to the White House and easily destroy the parasite? Were the parasite and its allies quailing in terror?

Grassemer's rationale for choosing Jack as his pawn was even worse than lying about Jack's supposed destiny. He had blatantly told Jack he had not been special before he was injected with magical water; Jack was only special because Grassemer made him special. Did Grassemer think that by giving Jack a purpose in life he would be absolved of his sins? Was this nothing more than a desperate attempt to vanquish the guilt he felt over abandoning the woman he loved and killing scores of magicians?

Jack pondered these questions until the car lurched to a sudden halt. Jack glanced out of the car window and saw they were parked beside another field, although this one was not full of cornstalks, but was barren except for a large tree trunk lying splintered on its side.

"Look, Jack. I'm sorry about lying to you," said Grassemer in a genuinely apologetic tone. "I believed I was doing the right thing. Let's just put it behind us and move on, okay?" Jack nodded grudgingly. "Now listen carefully," resumed Grassemer. "We're going to leave this car and sprint toward that tree trunk. We're going to hide behind it until a helicopter arrives. The helicopter, which will be manned by members of Walkrins, will escort us to the Walkrins' base. The helicopter should arrive soon, but in case anything happens, remember, you have to get to the chopper. Do you understand?"

Knowing he was in no position to argue, Jack nodded. On Grassemer's command, Jack wrenched the car door open and dashed across the field. Just as he was about to reach the tree trunk, Jack turned around, startled by the roar of an engine. He spotted the source of the noise, a black motorcycle skidding to a halt beside the blue sedan, driven by a portly man. Before Jack could get a better glimpse of the man, he felt powerful arms steering him behind the tree trunk, pushing him down to the ground as a series of deafening gunshots filled the air. Jack flattened his body against the ground, fear shooting through him as the sound of gunfire reverberated in his ears.

"Grassemer, what do we do?" hissed Jack as he lifted his head off the ground. Jack gave a horrified gasp as he caught sight of Grassemer, writhing on the ground, clutching the bleeding stump at the end of his right arm. "Oh my God, Grassemer, what—"

"He didn't hit my portal," muttered Grassemer through clenched teeth.

"What are you—" Jack stopped, realizing that Grassemer was not babbling delusional comments; he was assuring himself that his greatest weapon remained intact.

"Stay down. The helicopter will be here soon."

Between constricted, painful breaths, Grassemer slowly relinquished his grip from the torn flesh at the end of his right arm, perhaps realizing there was no way to stop the blood from flowing out of his body. For a moment, he started at the profusely bleeding stump, a dumbfounded expression crossing his face. He was no longer writhing; he was even lifting his body off the ground, his eyes locked on the place where his right hand had been only seconds before. Then his body began to violently tremble, his eyes brimming with tears.

"I swear on every drop of blood that taints my soul, I will kill Tom, the man who stole everything that made life worth living."

Grassemer's voice shook, the tears fell thick across his cheeks. Then without warning, he pulled himself off the ground, an anguished cry escaping his lips. With his remaining hand, he snatched his sword out of its sheath and charged at the lone man standing in the field.

The man standing before Grassemer was short and chubby with a bald head and bushy mustache. A rifle was slung over the man's right shoulder, a sword was belted at his side, and yet, his hands did not rest on either weapon. The man simply extended his left palm and aimed it at Grassemer. At first, nothing seemed to happen. Grassemer continued to charge, his sword clenched in his left hand, leaving a trail of blood behind him. Then the tree trunk behind which Jack was hiding, vanished. A second passed and then the tree trunk shot out of the man's palm. Grassemer rolled to the side before the tree trunk could crush him, his sword still grasped in his left hand. He then lifted himself off the ground and hurled his sword at his enemy's heart. The sword sailed through the air, the silver blade gleaming in the reddish tinge of the setting sun. The baldheaded man stared up at the weapon without moving his body out of harm's way. He calmly unsheathed his own sword and swatted Grassemer's weapon out of the air. Both men stayed still as they watched Grassemer's sword thud to the ground, as if entranced. A second passed, and then lava and gigantic boulders were flying through the air, spewing out of both men's portals.

"Grassemer!" screamed Jack, trying to call his mentor back before he entered the sea of oncoming natural resources.

As Jack watched Grassemer disappear from sight, his attention was diverted by a battered red truck zooming down the road, its tires screeching against the pavement as it came to a rickety stop next to the blue sedan and black motorcycle. Two men lumbered out of the truck, clutching pistols that they were aiming in Jack's direction. Not knowing what else to do, Jack frantically summoned lava, and launched it in the direction of the oncoming figures. But the lava did not reach the men with pistols. Instead, it sailed over their heads, landing on the opposite side of the road.

Jack scanned the field, initially flooded with relief, and then disgust as he spotted his attackers. They were not aiming their weapons at Jack anymore. They weren't even standing upright. Both of them were lying in pools of blood, their bodies mangled beyond recognition of anything humane. Jack couldn't understand how they had been killed so quickly, and by whom. That's when he heard the roar of the helicopter above him, saw three men holding machine guns, leaning out of the chopper. The sight of more guns initially frightened Jack before realizing these must be the people sent to escort Jack and Grassemer to the Walkrins' base.

Grassemer.

Jack whipped around, ashamed he had forgotten his mentor so easily. The baldheaded man was showering Grassemer with things summoned through magic: lava, ice, water, tree bark. With his other hand, the man attempted to slash Grassemer with his sword. Despite the ferocious attack and immense blood loss, Grassemer was still alive, dodging ice and lava, parrying the oncoming blows with his own magic. Jack couldn't figure how Grassemer could still be alive, how he still maintained the energy to fight. The sight of his strength, his refusal to submit, made Jack desperately wanted to help his mentor more than anything. But Jack had his orders, and there was no better way to obey Grassemer than to do as instructed. Jack tore his eyes away from the scene as he sprinted toward the helicopter and across the field. The helicopter had landed on the ground, enabling Jack to easily climb inside.

"Get behind us," barked one of the men as soon as Jack entered the inside of the helicopter.

Jack did as he was told, scrambling into a leather seat. Jack wildly glanced around the helicopter, seeing nothing but the back of the head of the helicopter's pilot, and a man with curly brown hair sitting next to him. As far as Jack could tell, he was unarmed.

"You're from Walkrins, right?" asked Jack desperately. The curly haired man nodded.

"I can't get a clear shot of Tom without harming Grassemer," said one of the men with a machine gun. Jack stood up, wanting to help Grassemer, but as soon as he moved, the man with the curly brown hair was pulling him back into his seat.

"Let go of me," insisted Jack.

"I can't. Grassemer's orders," said the man in an almost apologetic voice as he struggled to keep Jack down in his seat.

Jack was just about to summon something to break away from the curly haired man's grip when one of the men with machine guns said, "Grassemer's dead. Move the chopper in so we can get a clean shot on Tom."

"What!" yelped Jack, refusing to believe what he'd just heard. Jack felt the helicopter lift off the ground as he shouted for Grassemer.

As Jack finally broke free of the curly haired man's grasp, one of the men in front of him cried, "Reinforcements coming in. Target out of sight. Move out!"

Before Jack could get a glimpse of the ground below, confirm with his own eyes that Grassemer was dead, the sound of gunfire rekindled, this time all too close. Suddenly, one of the men with machine guns collapsed onto the helicopter floor, giving a tortured cry. Then, Jack felt powerful arms pull him back into his seat as he felt the sensation of a needle being jabbed into his arm. He slowly felt the world slide away from him as he slumped in his seat, shut off from reality.

CHAPTER 14

A group of disheveled looking men lay on a forest floor, their ragged clothes and haggard faces alight in the flickering flames of a dying fire. Many of them clutched empty whiskey bottles against their chests, all of them either passed out or asleep. Adjacent of the sleeping men was a figure shrouded in darkness, surveying the scene with keen eyes. Dick Wilkinson absentmindedly scratched his pencil thin mustache, his eyes still trained on the snoring men, searching for one in particular.

"My men would be unsettled by your prying eyes."

Dick wheeled around at the sound of the voice. A squat man with a bald head and bushy mustache leaned against the tree opposite of Dick, a flashlight illuminating his face. Dick's body relaxed as he recognized his longtime friend, the man he had come to see.

"It's good to see you, Tom," said Dick, extending his hand.

Tom eyed Dick's hand for a moment as if suspicious, and then returned the gesture. "What are you doing here? Surely you have some important place to be."

"I heard the news and knew I had to see you," said Dick.

Tom extended the palm of his hand, summoning a scrap of tree bark. He caught it in the air and began crunching it in his hand. "How'd you hear the news?"

"Master told me."

Tom nodded as he crouched down on the ground, pointing the flashlight at the base of a tree. Dick watched his friend, concerned by his odd behavior, disappointed that their meeting was not going as he had envisioned. He had imagined his friend would recount the battle, relive every moment of his victory.

"You've done a noble thing, Tom, ridding the world of a great evil," said Dick, determined to make Tom talk.

Tom continued to examine the base of the tree.

"Why are you so withdrawn? Do you feel guilty?"

"Of course not," replied Tom automatically.

"Then why are you acting this way?"

Tom finally stopped examining the tree, stood up, and faced Dick. "I'm worried that we're not accomplishing what we set out to do."

"How did killing Grassemer give you such thoughts? His death was above all what we wanted from the start. We're reconstructing civilization as it was meant to be. We're using our powers as we desire, not as dictated by superiors. Tom, we're the superior ones now, we're accomplishing everything we dreamed of doing. Have no doubts my friend. We're on the right track."

They stared at each other for a moment, Dick's face lit up with a smile while Tom continued to wear a blank expression. After a moment, Tom walked a few feet away from Dick. Before Dick could follow, Tom was back, now holding both a flashlight and a frayed black notebook.

"I retrieved this from Grassemer's car," said Tom, handing the notebook to Dick. "I'm sure Master will be interested to see it."

"Is this Roger Pucknee's journal?" asked Dick.

Tom nodded. Dick began to excitedly thumb through the journal, eager for his Master's reaction when he handed it over. Soon after opening the journal, Dick closed it, unable to read it in the dark, as a light wind began whistling through the night, sending a chill down his spine.

"Well, I need to head back now," said Dick, clutching the journal as if it was the key to heaven. "It was good seeing you. Hopefully we'll march into battle soon enough, the last battle against resistance." Dick paused. "By the way, Master wants you to not take any action until further notice. Just lay low. Notify your commanders of the same."

"I will."

Dick grinned, clapped his friend on the back, and began his trek out of the woods. His smile widened as he passed the decapitated head lying beside the fire, the eyes gazing up at him with unmistakable despair. Everything seemed to be falling into place.

Perfection could be the only result.

CHAPTER 15

The first thing Jack was aware of as his eyes fluttered open was the bright light shining down on him. He stared up at the light for a few seconds before turning away, his eyes stinging. As he turned his head, Jack saw he was in a room lined with beds. He felt his head resting upon a comfortable pillow, and white bed sheets were draped over his body. Only one other person was in a bed, a man who was sleeping a few beds away, but Jack could not see his face, for it was turned in the opposite direction. The room was silent except for the man's snores. Jack sat up, propping the pillow behind his head, glad that he was back in a proper bed instead of the backseat of Grassemer's blue sedan.

And then the memories flooded back into Jack's mind: Grassemer clutching the bloody stump at the end of his right arm, the two men lying in pools of their own blood, and the haunting words spoken by one of the men in the helicopter.

"Grassemer's dead."

The words reverberated in Jack's mind just like the gunfire that had reverberated in his ears. Anger and misery began clouding Jack's mind, sparking a fiery hate for those who killed his teacher. For a second, Jack was brought out of his simmering anger at the sound of a door creaking open. Standing in the doorway was a skinny man with curly brown hair. He held a briefcase in one hand and a laptop in the other. It took a moment for Jack to place the man, but he realized that it was the same man he had seen on the helicopter. The man looked at Jack, a bright smile lighting up his face as he said, "Ah, you've finally woken, Jack. Good, good, very good."

Jack noticed there was a sense of calm in the man's soft voice. He strode toward the bed Jack was lying in, placing his laptop and briefcase on a desk beside it.

Jack watched the man for a moment and then unable to help himself, burst out, "I don't mean to be rude or ignorant or anything, but who are you? Were you the guy holding me back on that helicopter? Where am I? What happened to me? Is Grassemer—?"

Jack could not finish. Somehow he felt that if he refused to say out loud what had happened, it might make things better.

The man pulled a chair up next to the bed, and clasped Jack's hands as he said in a gentle voice, "My name is Ryan Longring. I am honored to meet you, Jack Clark. I have heard of your father's great deeds and of your destiny."

At first Jack did not know what Ryan meant, but then he realized he was referring to the false perception that Jack was the only one who could destroy the parasite. Although Jack knew Ryan was trying to be comforting, he was only adding to Jack's misery. Grassemer's death was hard enough without contemplating the task he was believed destined to accomplish.

"I did hold you back on the helicopter," said Ryan. "Try not to be angry with me; I was only following Grassemer's orders. As to where you are, you are at the base of Walkrins. To be more specific, you are in the small hospital section of this place. As for what happened, that is much more complicated and tragic."

He paused, leaned in further, continuing to clasp Jack's hands. "As you may remember, Grassemer placed a phone call when you were in the car. He was calling for help. We were to follow the orders we had been given if you and Grassemer were attacked or in danger during your training. Three gunmen, a pilot, and I flew in our helicopter to rescue the two of you. By the time we arrived, Grassemer was already under heavy attack from Tom. We wanted to help him, but we feared that an inaccurate shot would accidentally hit Grassemer. Sadly, it didn't matter in the end. Our gunmen took out the two men working for Tom before they could kill you. You reached the helicopter, but naturally you couldn't sit still while Grassemer was in danger. I had to restrain you. Tom, the man Grassemer was fighting, killed him before we could do anything. We tried to then move in and take out Tom, but reinforcements arrived and we were forced to flee. You were obviously traumatized by Grassemer's death, so I gave you heavy sedation."

Ryan let go of Jack's hands and began typing into his laptop. "Updating the status of your condition," explained Ryan, "you've been asleep for over twenty-four hours." He stopped typing for a moment and turned back to Jack, wearing a sorrowful expression. "I'm really sorry, Jack. Grassemer was a great man. He will be sorely missed."

As Ryan spoke, it dawned on Jack what had truly happened. Nothing mattered anymore. Grassemer was dead, and Jack would never hear his mentor's words of wisdom again.

Jack glanced around the room, trying to divert his thoughts elsewhere. He saw that the man in the other bed was sitting up now and he and Ryan were talking together in low voices. He was an elderly man with a bald head and a clean-shaven face. Something had happened to the man's right eye, or around that area of his face, it was caked in dry blood and covered in thick bandages. Ryan walked back over to his briefcase and opened it up, revealing a basic set of medical instruments.

"Ryan, who is that that guy over there and what happened to him?" asked Jack quietly.

Ryan gave Jack a sad look. "That is Tony, one of the best gunmen in Walkrins, and one of the courageous men who helped save you. Before we retreated, he was shot in the right eye by one of Tom's men. He is now completely blind in that eye."

Ryan turned around and strode over to Tony's bed with his medical instruments in hand. Jack had not thought things could get any worse, and now he was hearing this man would never see anything out of his right eye because he helped save Jack. Two weeks ago no one but his mom had cared about him. What had happened, what had changed? Now people were suffering and jeopardizing their lives for Jack, a fat, pimply boy who had been the victim of high school bullying, who they honestly believed would destroy their greatest enemy: the parasite with human intelligence.

CHAPTER 16

There was a knock on the door and Ryan said in his calm voice, "Come in."

A man walked into the room who looked only a few years older than Jack. He had blonde hair which came down to about his ears and a smooth facial complexion. He was wearing jeans and a white t-shirt which partially exposed his muscular arms. He walked over to Tony's bed. "How ya feeling, man?" he asked.

"I'm doin' all right, Freddy, I'm doin' okay," said Tony. "I'm in a helluva lotta pain, but hey, better to lose one eye than both. I've always been left-handed so now I can just say the left side of my body is the strongest, eh?"

"Power to the lefties," chuckled the blonde-haired man.

"Amen, brother!"

"I'd like to keep talking, Tony, but I gotta go talk with Jack Clark," said the blonde-haired man, nodding his head in Jack's direction.

"Jack's here?" The blonde-haired man nodded and Tony cried out, "Hello, Jack, hello! Sorry I didn't speak to you before. Couldn't see you." Tony smiled and pointed to his eye. "My name's Tony."

"It's an honor to meet you, Tony. I'm really sorry about your eye, it's my fault, if I wasn't such a—"

"My boy, it is an honor to meet *you*. You are the one who will destroy the parasite and end this infernal war. Don't be sorry, my eyesight in my left eye is far better than my right anyway. Besides, losing you would be much worse than losing an eye."

Something is wrong here, thought Jack quizzically. *How can this man who I've never met before now be willing to be partially blind so I can survive?*

"Hey, Jack, I haven't introduced myself yet. I'm Fred Waxston," said the blonde-haired man as he walked over to Jack's bed and shook his hand.

"Nice to meet you. I'm Jack Clark."

"We already know who you are, kiddo."

Fred grinned at Jack. Jack tried to smile back, but he couldn't. He was too encumbered by misery. All he wanted to do was press his face against the pillow, close his eyes, and fall back to sleep. Somehow, Jack knew this wasn't an option. Perhaps it was because he'd been asleep for over a day, or maybe it was the fact that Ryan, Fred, and Tony all had their eyes trained on Jack, as if expecting him to do something incredible. The only thing that happened was Jack's stomach giving a loud growl.

"Uh, is there any food I could have?" asked Jack. If he wasn't going to sleep, the only other thing to do was eat.

Fred chuckled. "Yeah, follow me. I'll also give you a tour of this place."

"Sounds good," said Jack, glad to have a distraction from thinking about Grassemer's death and the loss of Tony's right eye.

"Follow me," said Fred, walking toward the door. As Jack lifted himself out of his bed he realized that someone had changed his clothes; he now wore a blue Penn State football t-shirt and jeans which definitely did not belong to him.

Before leaving, Jack turned around and said, "Thanks for patching me up Ryan, and it was nice meeting you Tony."

"My pleasure," said Ryan as he stowed away his medical instruments in his briefcase.

"I'll see you 'round, Jack!" said Tony enthusiastically.

Fred opened the door, and Jack went through murmuring thanks to Fred. As Jack stepped out of the hospital room, he found himself standing in a hallway with concrete walls, a concrete ceiling, and a concrete floor. One side of the hallway was lined with rows of mahogany doors with numbers pinned to them. The other side contained a black iron railing that stretched across the full length of the hallway. Jack walked over to the railing and peered over the edge. Below was a wide entrance hall with a marble floor, supported by towering marble pillars. A lit chandelier hung from the center of the ceiling, illuminating the marble hall that appeared devoid of any human presence. Jack stared down at the entrance hall for a few seconds before Fred tapped him on the shoulder, asking to move on. Jack followed Fred down the end of the hallway, toward a metal door that led to a flight of stairs.

After only going down one story and through another metal door, Jack found himself standing next to Fred in a large concrete room jam-packed with square tables. Each table was surrounded by plain black chairs. At the back of the room, there was a door with a bright red sign hanging above it, reading *Emergency Exit*.

"This is where everyone eats. The kitchen is over there," said Fred, indicating a pair of swinging white doors.

At that moment, the doors swung open and two men emerged carrying a jumble of trays, plates, and silverware. One of the men was in a wheelchair, yet he was able to transport a pile of silverware in his lap while he navigated his wheelchair with his free hands.

"Why do we always get the late shift?" grumbled the man who was not in the wheelchair. This man had a beer belly, a balding head with a few wisps of black hair, and a deep tan.

"It ain't so bad, Ricardo, in fact, I kinda like working late," said the man in the wheelchair, who looked quite similar to Ricardo except he was not nearly as chubby.

"Easy for you to say, Juan, all you've got is a handful of silverware whereas I'm holdin' all these trays and—" Ricardo swore as several of the plates he was holding fell out of his hands and smashed against the floor. "Now I'm going to have to spend my whole night cleaning this mess. I was hoping to get a good night's sleep, but nooooo! I have to be given the late shift as usual."

"Good evening, Ricardo and Juan," said Fred politely as Ricardo began to sweep the broken plates into a bin with a broom. Juan looked up and began to wheel his wheelchair over to where Fred and Jack were standing.

"How nice of you to stop by, Fred. I see you've brought a friend." He grinned. "A newbie by the looks of it, eh?"

"This is not just any new member of Walkrins. This is Jack Clark, the one who is destined to destroy the parasite. His father was one of the founders of Walkrins, as you should know."

"Yes, yes, of course I know. I personally knew his father," said Juan, putting down his lapful of silverware on a nearby table. "I'm delighted to meet you, Jack. I am no fighter like Fred and many others. My talent is cooking. That's my brother, Ricardo," said Juan, pointing over to his brother who was still grumbling over the plates he had dropped and having to work the night shift. "We are cooks of Walkrins. With so many people here that have to eat, someone has to make food. That is the job of my brother and me along with several others. Golish works us overtime because we're the only decent cooks. I'm fine with it but as you can see Ricardo is not."

"What'd you just say about me?" called Ricardo from across the dining hall.

"Nothing!" shouted Juan in exasperation. He turned back to Jack and Fred. "Now what can I do for you gentlemen?"

"Jack would like some food," said Fred.

"Well, you've come to the right place. We have leftovers from tonight's dinner. Are tacos fine with you?" Jack nodded. "I'll be right back, then." Juan wheeled himself over to his brother. "Ricardo, forget the dishes. We have an important guest to serve." Ricardo grumbled something unintelligible and followed his brother back into the kitchen. Jack followed Fred over to one of the square tables where they sat down.

"So what do you think of our base so far, Jack?" asked Fred.

Jack shrugged. Hunger, misery, and thoughts of Grassemer had sapped curiosity out of him for the time being. "It doesn't seem like much of a rebel base to me," said Jack.

"That wasn't the initial purpose. This hotel was built as a sort of experiment. It was supposed to be a getaway in the mountains, an escape from reality. The architects tried really hard to make it unique and appealing. You'll see what I mean when we continue the tour. But the plan didn't work. People didn't want to take vacation in a mountain in central Pennsylvania. The transportation was inconvenient anyway, having to take a helicopter into the mountain." Fred paused. "So the hotel was abandoned. No one bothered to tear it down. I mean, they weren't going to do anything with a hotel in the mountains. So when our parents arrived along with Golish, the hotel was in great condition." Jack gave Fred a blank stare. "Your father and my mom and dad," said Fred. "They found this place with Gregory Golish. Didn't Grassemer tell you about that?"

"Yeah, he did. Sorry, if I don't seem to be paying attention with what you're saying, I am listening. I just feel…" Jack trailed off, not wanting to share the fact that the sound of Grassemer's anguished cry was ringing in his head.

"It's okay. I understand what you're going through. My parents—well, Grassemer probably told you what happened to them."

Waxston. That's when Jack remembered. Fred's parents had been killed while trying to assassinate Dick Wilkinson. No, his mother had been killed, but his father had been turned into a Joinx. Jack tried to imagine what it would be like to know that his mother was still alive, but that she wouldn't recognize her own son, or even know who she was. Her past obliterated, her identity gone. It seemed almost worse than death. Jack looked back at Fred with a newfound sense of respect, realizing what Fred had to deal with, that he had most likely faced many more hardships than Jack. Yet here he sat, seeming happy and at ease.

The doors to the kitchen swung open and Juan and Ricardo reappeared, Ricardo bearing a plate of tacos, Juan wheeling toward the table with napkins and a bottle of water in his lap. "Here ya go," mumbled Ricardo, placing the plate in front of Jack.

"Thank you," said Jack.

"No problem," said Juan, handing Jack the bottle of water and napkins.

Juan situated his wheelchair beside the table while his brother went back to cleaning up the broken plates on the floor. Jack wolfed down the tacos, his hunger giving way to manners. Jack was so intent on eating that he had not noticed that Fred and Juan had been watching him the whole time.

Troubled by their silence, Jack decided to initiate conversation. "So if you're living in this hotel up in the mountains, how do you get ingredients for tacos?"

"We make trips to nearby towns and stores," said Fred. "Sometimes we take our helicopter and park it away from the town so we don't draw any attention. Other times we just walk down the mountain and then along the highway until we reach a store. That's not preferable, though, because then we have to lug all the food up the mountain."

Not knowing what else to say, Jack plucked one of the napkins off the table and wiped the corners of his mouth, the red color of the smeared salsa reminding him of the profusely bleeding stump protruding from Grassemer's arm. The image swam before his eyes, Grassemer clutching the bleeding stump as his body began to violently tremble. Jack tried to rid his mind of the image, or at least focus on something else, but it refused to budge. He was on the verge of shouting at the nauseating image to go away before he looked up and saw Fred and Juan peering at him curiously.

"Those tacos were delicious," said Jack in an excessively complimentary voice.

"I'm glad you thought so," said Juan.

"Well, I'm going to continue giving Jack a tour, if that's all right with you," said Fred.

Jack nodded in agreement as he stood up, taking a final swig of his bottle of water.

"Thanks for everything," said Jack.

"It was nothing," said Juan, waving a hand.

With that, Jack and Fred bade Juan farewell, and exited the dining hall. They were now walking through another hallway, this one lined with doors on both sides with no black railing. After only walking a few feet down the hallway, Fred stopped in front of a set of thick oak doors. He pushed open the door, and both he and Jack went inside. As they entered the room, Jack saw something he had not expected: a basketball court. It was empty except for a bin of basketballs lying next to one of the free throw lines.

"I definitely didn't expect this," said Jack in surprise.

"This was supposed to be one of the hotel's appeals," said Fred. "I guess the architects didn't consider that someone would rather play basketball for free in their backyard than pay to take a helicopter and play basketball in the mountains. But I'm glad they built it, basketball's good fun and exercise." Fred walked over to the bin of basketballs, took one out, and sunk a shot from behind the three-point line.

"You're pretty good," said Jack.

"I try to shoot around or play a game at least three times a week," said Fred, shrugging. "Hey, we should play sometime."

"I'm not very good at sports."

"It doesn't matter. We'll just have a good time."

Both Fred and Jack gazed around a little longer and then Fred said, "There's other means of exercise if you're not a basketball person. In that room," he pointed his finger at a door to the side of the court "there's an elliptical, a treadmill, weights, that kind of stuff. Unless you want to see it, can we move on with the tour?" Jack nodded as Fred tossed the basketball back into the bin, walked to the entrance, and shut the oak doors.

Only after a few seconds of walking, Fred stopped in front of another set of doors, this time made of metal. Above the doors was a sign that read *Fighting Complex*.

"Fighting Complex?" inquired Jack.

"It used to be the hotel ballroom. Now it's where Walkrins' members go to practice swordplay, shooting with a gun, or any other means of fighting. Here, I'll show you the inside."

Fred heaved open the heavy metal doors. Jack walked in and began to survey the Fighting Complex. The room was covered in soft, flat yellow mattresses that Jack guessed were there to cushion any falls during fights. Several wooden dummies were lined up against the wall which Jack could tell were used for sword practice. Some of the dummies' body parts hung lopsidedly, the wood splintered and covered in scratch marks. A series of targets and bullseyes were lined up against the wall, which were most likely used for shooting practice. There were several bins and barrels of wooden swords. Jack had expected to see all different kinds of eccentric weapons, but it appeared that the wooden practice swords were the only weapons in the whole room. The Fighting Complex was quite spacious; it was a large room with lots of empty space for dueling and practicing with other weapons.

The room was empty except for a young woman and a middle-aged man who were dueling in the center of the room with the wooden practice swords. As Jack and Fred entered the room, the woman looked away from the man she was practicing with to see who the newcomers were. This slight moment of hesitation gave the middle-aged man the chance to stab her in the stomach, but he didn't do any real damage, the tips of the wooden swords were blunt.

"Don't let anything distract you," said the man as the young woman began to fight him again. "If this was a real fight I would have killed you. You must remain focused on the fight at hand, nothing else exists."

The young woman was now fighting aggressively. There were several times where Jack was positive that she was going to hit at least a part of him, but he continued to parry every attack she tried to make. Meanwhile, she was unable to block any of his blows.

After about ten minutes of this, the woman panted, "It's getting late, Rax. I think I've had enough. You're impossible to beat."

"I have weaknesses just like the next man."

"Or woman."

"Or woman," repeated the man in a deadly serious voice.

Fred beckoned Jack to walk forward and called over, "I'd hate to think how I'd do against you, Rax. Rachel destroys me every time I practice with her."

"I was doing well until *you* came along. You got me all distracted." said Rachel, smiling.

"I'm a distraction because I'm such an enthralling person. You just couldn't help looking at me." Rachel chuckled at Fred's comment as she pushed her blonde hair out of her face. "Jack, this is my girlfriend, Rachel Holmes," said Fred, beaming at her.

Rachel was tall and slender, had an attractive face, and a clear complexion like her boyfriend. Her most striking feature was her long, honey blonde hair braided in a ponytail. She looked to be about the same age as Fred, which meant she was a few years older than Jack. A wave of jealousy washed over Jack at the thought of this gorgeous, nice girl being engaged in a romantic relationship with Fred.

"How do you do?" asked Jack, politely sticking out his hand to shake.

Rachel giggled as she shook Jack's hand. "I do fine, thank you very much. You're quite the gentleman, Jack. You should give Fred lessons, he seriously lacks manners." There was an awkward pause in which Jack was not sure how to respond to Rachel's comment, but the moment was broken as Fred and Rachel began to laugh hysterically.

"And this," said Fred, still chuckling, "is Robert Rax. He's the best swordsman I've ever met, and do you know who taught him? Your father, Jason, who, you may not know, was quite a swordsman himself."

Rax looked like he was in his mid thirties. He was average height, and was extremely skinny which Jack supposed came from constant sword practice. Jack noticed his head and face were entirely clean-shaven.

"It's an honor to meet you," said Jack, holding out his hand for Rax to shake.

"Pleasure to meet you as well," said Rax, giving Jack a firm handshake.

"Hopefully I will get the opportunity to teach you swordplay. Grassemer may have taught you the ways of magic, but you need more than magic to fight. You need a tangible weapon. Now if you will excuse me, I'm going to go to bed." Rax strode over to the barrel of wooden swords, deposited his into the barrel, and walked out of the metal doors. Rax had not smiled or laughed once during the conversation, his face had remained impassive the entire time.

"You'll love Rax once you get to know him," said Rachel. "He's not one to have a good laugh with, but he's a brilliant swordsman."

"Not to mention he had a somewhat difficult past before he came to Walkrins," said Fred vaguely.

"I'm going to go back to the room now," said Rachel as she stowed her wooden sword in the same barrel. Fred nodded and went to open the metal doors for Rachel and Jack. "Good night, Jack, it was a pleasure meeting you. I hope to see you around," said Rachel. She pecked Fred on the cheek and then walked down the hallway. Jack and Fred both gazed at her until she was out of sight.

"Over here," said Fred, taking Jack back to reality as he pointed at a wooden chestnut door across from the Fighting Complex, "is our library. It was supposed to be the intellectual draw for guests."

Fred pried open the door, revealing the inside. The library was only a quarter of the size of the Fighting Complex. The room contained three bookshelves crammed with books, a checkout desk, and a circle of red armchairs in the corner.

"I'm not much of a reader, but Rachel is, so I've been going here far more than I would like recently," said Fred. "You can take a book anytime you want. If there's no one at the checkout desk, you just have to leave a note saying what book you checked out, who you are, and the date. Several of our members work here each day organizing the books. Some of the books were already here; some of them are donated by new members."

Jack, who often didn't read for English class, found the library to be the least interesting room he had seen so far. Yet Jack suspected that this room had been Grassemer's favorite. He imagined his teacher sitting in one of the red armchairs, immersed in a book of his choice. It was probably his one escape from reality, an escape from murder, betrayal, horrific memories, and the daunting future.

"Are you ready to move on?" asked Fred, bringing Jack out of his thoughts. Jack nodded and walked out of the library. Fred did not take Jack behind anymore of the doors in the hallway. They continued walking until they reached the marble entrance hall that Jack had spotted from behind the black iron railing. Jack walked over to one of the towering pillars and observed it, his hands running over the smooth surface. Jack gazed up and saw five floors of hallways, lined with mahogany doors and black railings.

"We were on the second floor earlier, the first hallway with a black railing," said Fred. "To give you a recap of the tour, the first floor contains the dining hall, the kitchen, the basketball court, the exercise room, the Fighting Complex, the library, storage rooms I didn't show you, and this entrance hall. Floors two through six are mainly bedrooms except for the hospital on the second floor and the camera room on the sixth floor.

There is one flight of stairs you can access on every floor; down here it leads to the dining hall. There's also an elevator you can take, but you have to go through the kitchen." Jack walked away from the pillar and toward the end of the entrance hall where a set of metal doors stood. "Those doors lead to outside the hotel," said Fred. "You can only leave when it's light out. And you can never go alone, you must always be accompanied."

The wide expanse of the marble hall made Jack feel insignificant, just the way he had felt for most of his life, before Grassemer's lie.

"Hey, do I have a room to stay in?" asked Jack, wanting to bury himself yet again in sleep.

"A room has been set aside for you on the fifth floor. Follow me." Jack and Fred walked out of the marble entrance hall, and made their way back to the staircase. After climbing several flights of stairs, they reached the fifth floor where Fred stopped in front of one of the mahogany doors, with the number 511 pinned to it. Fred withdrew a silver key from his pocket and slid it into the lock. It clicked open, allowing them to enter.

The room was in pristine condition. A neatly made bed stood in the center. A lamp and a digital alarm clock were situated on a nightstand next to the bed. There was also a private bathroom with a sparkling clean floor, sink, and shower.

"The architects built us everything we needed," said Fred, smiling. "All we have to do now is keep the water and electricity running." Fred walked over to the nightstand and opened a drawer attached to it. "Inside here is a week's worth of clothes. You've been provided with appropriate wear for all occasions." Fred closed the drawer and handed the silver key to Jack. "This is the key to your room. I'll come get you in the morning because I need to take you to Golish's office. Just so you know, breakfast is served from eight to nine. Lunch is from twelve to one. Dinner is from six to eight. Any more questions?"

"No, but thanks for showing me around. I'd be lost without you."

"It was nothing, honestly. I've lived here my whole life so I should know my way around, right?" said Fred with a slight chuckle.

"So I guess I'll see you tomorrow morning," said Jack.

"Sounds like a plan. You know, it was great to meet you at last. You're exactly what Walkrins needs to win this war. Have a good night, Jack." Fred flashed Jack another smile, and departed from the room.

Tired from standing, Jack sunk onto the bed. His thoughts drifted to all the people he had met in this one night: Ryan, Tony, Fred, Juan, Ricardo, Rax, and Rachel. Jack knew he should feel nothing but appreciation for the kindness they had shown him. But the only emotion he could identify at that moment was hate, hate toward Grassemer for lying, and hate toward Tom, the man who killed Grassemer.

CHAPTER 17

Jack woke with a start the next morning as Fred pounded on his door. "Wake up, Jack! We gotta get some breakfast before your appointment with Golish."

Jack blearily opened his eyes, groaning at the sound of Fred's voice. Even though he had slept for twenty-four hours and then went to bed again, he felt exhausted. He attributed this to the anguish of recent events and that he had only slept for two hours in his new room. The whole scene of Grassemer's death had been playing over and over again in his mind as he tried to fall asleep. Closing his eyes meant seeing Grassemer's bleeding stump. Opening his eyes only showed darkness. And all the while, Grassemer's agonizing cries rang in his ears.

After brushing his teeth and getting dressed, Jack walked down to the dining hall for breakfast. Most of the square tables were now occupied. Food was already placed on the tables. Jack spotted Fred sitting at a nearby table and went to join him. As soon as Jack sat down, he starting grabbing everything he could reach: bacon, donuts, chocolate chip muffins, and waffles which he drenched in syrup.

"This is a nicer breakfast than usual," said Fred who seemed to be thoroughly enjoying his donut with chocolate icing and red sprinkles. "Usually we just have cereal and toast. I suppose Ricardo, Juan and the other cooks wanted to give you a good first-ever Walkrins' breakfast." Fred gobbled up the rest of his donut and reached for another.

After both Fred and Jack ate all they could, Fred led Jack to Golish's office which was located on the opposite end of Jack's room on the fifth floor. The first thing Jack noticed as he approached Golish's office was that the door was flanked by two huge men who looked as if they had previously been sumo wrestlers. They each held an axe which they crossed over the door as Fred and Jack approached.

"Who goes there?" questioned the guard on the left.

"It is I, Fred Waxston, here to escort Jack Clark who has an appointment with Mr. Golish."

"You may enter," said both men in unison, in deep, rumbling voices. They lowered their axes and opened the door, allowing Fred and Jack to pass.

"What was that all about?" murmured Jack after the door was shut behind them.

"They're Golish's bodyguards. It's common knowledge that our enemies have infiltrated this place with a spy. As our leader, and the only surviving founder, Golish needs protection. Obviously it would be suicide to try to get past those guys, so he's well protected."

As they entered Golish's office, Jack saw that somebody was already meeting with him. Sitting in a chair across from Golish (who was sitting behind his desk) was the woman who Jack had dreamed was at the Lincoln Memorial, and was chased by the Joinxs. Grassemer said her name was Sarah Setter.

"Sarah," said Fred in surprise, "you're back."

"Yep," said Sarah, leaning back in her chair. "I just got back a few hours ago." Jack had thought that Rachel was one of the most beautiful girls he had ever seen, but Sarah was serious competition. She was tall and slender like Rachel. Sarah also had long hair, but it was black instead of blonde. Her face was even more attractive than Rachel's, and she was far tanner, although it wasn't the type of tan Ricardo and Juan had.

"Sarah," said Golish from his chair, "I would like to introduce you to the newest member of Walkrins, Jack Clark." Sarah stood up from her chair and walked over to Jack with a mesmerized look on her face.

"So, it is truly you," she said in a barely audible whisper.

"What do you mean?" asked Jack, who couldn't understand why she seemed so captivated by him.

"I heard rumors. But are you really the only one who can destroy the parasite?"

Now Jack understood why she was so interested in him. Then it struck Jack that perhaps the only reason everyone had been so friendly, the only reason he had been so warmly welcomed was because of this ridiculous rumor that Grassemer had created, and perhaps the fact his father had been a founder of Walkrins. Did anyone truly care about Jack, or were they just trying to be on good terms with the son of the brave Jason Clark, and the one who would supposedly end the war?

"Yes, the rumors are true," said Jack flatly. A twinge of remorse nabbed at him as he told the lie. He stared into her pale blue eyes, letting the color distract him from his guilt. Sarah continued to look at him as if he was the most fascinating person she had ever met.

"I would love to speak to Grassemer, where is he at the moment?" asked Sarah without looking away from Jack.

"Sarah," said Golish, his voice shaking, "Grassemer is dead. Tom killed him."

"What?" said Sarah incredulously. She spun around and stared at Golish uncomprehendingly, yet Jack knew she had understood him perfectly. It was not incomprehension on her face, but shock and despair. Tears slid down her smooth cheeks, causing similar emotions to stir within Jack. "May I be excused, Golish?" she choked through her tears.

"You may," muttered Golish who looked as if he too might begin crying at any moment. "You can leave as well, Fred. Jack will be fine with me." Fred nodded and left the room with Sarah.

Golish looked as if he had not slept or groomed himself in weeks. He had a black, scraggly beard, in addition to untidy black hair. Deep bags hung under his eyelids, making his eyes look heavy. His desk was covered in a jumble of papers, which gave Jack the impression he was also disorganized. Jack's attention was most drawn to Golish's outfit; he wore a wrinkled white t-shirt and plaid pajama pants, not the typical clothes of rebel leaders.

"Sorry for the mess, Jack. I'm usually not like this, but it's been so chaotic lately. In only a matter of weeks, three of the five founders of Walkrins have died, three of my dearest friends. Money and food are scarcer than ever. We grow weaker and our enemies grow stronger. The spy who has infiltrated our base continues to convey valuable information to the parasite, and I fear an attack on this place is inevitably close. But at least we were able to save you," finished Golish with a weak smile.

It took Jack a moment to comprehend Golish's last statement. "Do you mean that you were—?"

"Yes, I was one of the gunmen."

"Thanks for saving me," said Jack, trying to sound grateful.

"I should be the one thanking you. You survived the attack, which is more important to the outcome of this war than you realize." Then, after a pause, "We wanted to recover Grassemer's body, but—"

"It doesn't matter," Jack cut in. "Grassemer told me that he believed the body is merely a shell that holds the mind and soul of every individual. His body is now just an empty shell; he wouldn't care what happens to it." Golish gazed at Jack intently, yet Jack had a funny feeling Golish was not thinking about him.

"You remind me of your father. He would always quote other people, particularly Grassemer. Your father was a great man. Grassemer probably told you I used to be a drug addict. No one ever wanted to give me a chance, except for your father. He saw the good in me, which no one else, including me saw. A day hasn't gone by that I don't think of him. He was an extraordinary man, one of a kind. There were times when everything would seem hopeless, but your father always remained positive." Golish stared past Jack, his mind in a different world.

"Hopefully there will be a time when I can tell you more about your father, but unfortunately, we have other matters. First, I must know how competent of a magician you are. I want an apple."

Jack extended his left hand and directed it at Golish. An apple flew out of it which Golish caught in midair.

"I want five apples. Summon them slowly; I want to be able to catch each one individually."

Jack kept his hand in the same position, and did as he was told.

"It's been weeks since I last washed my face, so how about a nice splash of water?"

Water surged out of Jack's palm as Golish's face was doused.

"You can stop now," sputtered Golish. He shook his head, causing water to splay onto Jack and on his desk. "Well, you seem like a good enough magician. Of course, Grassemer taught you well." Golish paused as he fingered his wet beard. "What did you think of Grassemer?"

"It's hard to say."

Golish chortled. "I know what you mean. Grassemer was a tricky guy. You're fortunate that you spent nearly two weeks with him. Aside from your father, Fred's parents, me, and you, he hardly ever spent time with anyone. Sometimes he would disappear for months without telling anyone what he was up to. We should consider ourselves lucky that he considered us worthy of his time. The world is far worse off without him."

Golish sighed and absentmindedly ran his fingers through his rumpled hair as he stared at the ceiling. This went on for several minutes, until Golish caught sight of Jack staring at him.

"Let's get back to business," said Golish, suddenly adopting an authoritative tone. "You seem proficient with magic, but you also need to learn to fight otherwise. I want you to learn swordplay with Robert Rax everyday in the Fighting Complex, from two to five in the afternoon. Rax learned swordplay from your father, and he is the best swordsman Walkrins currently has. You have no other obligations while here, other than providing the cooks with fruits and vegetables." Golish paused yet again as he scratched his nose. "These are difficult times, but try to enjoy yourself. There is plenty to do here. Do you have any questions or comments about what I have asked you to do?"

"I have two questions. Is there going to be a funeral or memorial service for Grassemer? Also, what's the story behind Sarah?"

"Well, to answer your first question, there isn't going to be a funeral or memorial service. As I told you, we didn't recover his body, and Grassemer forbade us from doing anything of the sort if he died. He said it would be a waste of time for Walkrins and that our focuses should be directed on fighting and destroying the parasite. As for Sarah, we found her lying on the side of a highway when she was a baby. Her parents, whoever they are, just abandoned her, I guess. A kind, elderly couple called the Setters who were longtime members of Walkrins adopted her. They raised her and turned her into the fine young lady she is. Sadly, a few years back, the Setters tragically died of heart attacks around the same time. Now, Sarah is like any other member of Walkrins, doing anything she can to defeat the parasite. Do you have any more questions?"

"Yeah, is there any way I can contact my mother?"

"Here, I have a cell phone," said Golish. He reached into a cluster of papers and pulled out a dingy old cell phone. "It was a good phone back in the day," said Golish almost defensively. Jack murmured his thanks as Golish handed him the phone and he dialed his mom's cell phone number. A series of ringing ensued, but Susan Clark did not pick up her phone. "Hi, this is Susan Clark. I'm not available right now, so please leave your name and number after the beep. Thanks!"

"Hi, Mom, this is Jack. I don't know if you got my last message or not. I hope everything is going well. Also, we have a lot to talk about." Jack racked his brains, feeling like he wanted to say more, but nothing else came to mind. "So, call me back on this cell phone as soon as you can. Thanks, bye."

Jack snapped the cell phone shut and handed it back to Golish.

"If she calls back, I'll tell you immediately," said Golish reassuringly.

"Thanks," said Jack, trying to sound relieved.

"Sure thing. So, do you have any more questions?"

Jack shook his head.

"Very well, then. I'll walk you back to your room."

As Jack stood up to leave, he spotted a newspaper lying in the heap of papers on Golish's desk. The newspaper had caught his eye because Jack saw a picture of himself atop the front page. Glancing at Golish who had his back turned, Jack snatched the newspaper off the table and shoved it into the right pocket of his jeans.

Golish held open the door for Jack. The two sumo wrestler bodyguards stood aside as Jack and Golish passed the threshold.

"What do you think of them?" muttered Golish as he jerked his thumb back at the sumo wrestler guards.

"I'm sure they do their job well," said Jack, unsure of how else to respond.

"You got that right."

The rest of the walk was silent until they reached the door to Jack's room.

"It was a pleasure to meet you, Jack. Make sure you drop by my office sometime so we can talk about your father." Golish shook Jack's hand, and walked back in the opposite direction.

CHAPTER 18

Once inside his room, Jack lay down on his bed and began to read the newspaper article with his picture next to it. The headline read: **Locals bothered by teenager's disappearance**. Bracing himself for the worst, Jack began to read.

Sixteen-year-old Jack Clark has disappeared. Clark was last seen by his mother, Susan Clark, on Saturday morning.

"I saw him before I left for my business trip," she said. "I have no idea where he is now." Clark's mother refused to further comment on her son's disappearance.

Local police have been searching for Clark since his disappearance was discovered on the following Monday morning when he did not arrive at school.

"There was no sign of struggle at his home," said local police Chief Arnold Owens. "We don't think this is a case of kidnapping. It's more likely he left of his accord." Owens admitted that the police have no lead on where Clark disappeared to.

Clark's physical education teacher, Linda Kurbik, doesn't think Clark left with a destination in mind. "He has a habit of wandering off," she explained. "Last Friday, during class, he walked into the forest behind our school. It took me the whole class period to find him. I just hope the poor darling hasn't gotten himself into any trouble."

Although it is unclear what Clark's home life is like, his classmates feel sure that his disappearance has nothing to do with wanting to escape school. "Everyone here is really nice to him," said Trent Owens, a classmate of Clark's, and son of police Chief Owens. "My friends and I always go out of our way to say hi to him, you know, make sure he knows we like him, even if he is odd."

Clark's best friend, Ashley Fletcher, tearfully expressed her sadness over Clark's disappearance. "I'm so worried about him," said Fletcher between wrenching sobs. "We've always been there for each other, but now, I'm not there for him. I feel like such a bad friend."

Police are continuing to search for Clark, but in the meantime, citizens are urged to call their local police number if they see Clark, pictured on the right.

Jack finished the article, fuming. He saw the newspaper was dated five days after he had been in the cornfield with Grassemer. Enraged, Jack crumpled the paper, and hurled it into the wastebasket next to his nightstand.

CHAPTER 19

Jack went down to lunch as early as he could; he wanted to avoid thinking about the article he had read. Seeing his mother's words brought on aching pain, pain that would only diminish when he was reunited with her. The only good thing about the article was the fact that if she had really been interviewed by the journalist who wrote the story, it meant she was fine. Then again, she could have made those comments as a prisoner of the parasite. Or maybe she was now a prisoner, but not when the article was written. There was also the possibility of unethical journalists creating fake quotations. That would explain why her comments were so brief and almost uncaring, so unlike Susan Clark.

The possibilities were endless. But all that mattered to Jack was that she was all right, protected by members of Walkrins as Grassemer promised, and conducting her business meetings without fear of the parasite or its minions.

Although increased worry for his mother came from reading the article, there was something just as upsetting: the insolent lies from Trent, Ms. Kurbik, and Ashley. As Jack walked down the fifth floor hallway, it struck him that he didn't care if the parasite or its allies ever killed anyone from his old school. He began imagining how he would hurt them if he ever got the chance, those fiends who made life so miserable for him.

For Trent, it would be a bullet through the head. No, that was too merciful. First, his arms would be cut off, those burly arms he was so proud of. Then, the legs would be chopped off. As blood seeped from the spots that once held his appendages, Trent would slowly die from blood loss, his once fine physique tarnished by mutilation.

Next would be Ms. Kurbik. Her tongue would be cut out and her lips scraped off her face. No more screaming for her. To add insult to injury, a baseball would be stuffed in her disfigured mouth. Her nose would be plugged. Tied to the trees on the edge of the school baseball field, with her breathing cut off, Ms. Kurbik would slowly suffocate to death.

The third victim would be Ashley. That arrogant girl who thought her good looks made her superior to the ugly Jack Clark. The first step would be to damage her hair, that short burgundy hair she tended to so diligently, that she washed and combed and straightened and applied expensive shampoos to every morning and night. It would be completely shaved off. She would be forced to walk past all the boys at school, who would laugh at her, the repugnant bald girl. Once she had been publicly humiliated, she would be tied to a wooden post in an isolated area. Her clothes would be ripped off her body. Then she would be whipped until her once fair skin had transformed into hunks of bloody flesh. She would be abandoned, still tied to the wooden post. If she didn't die from blood loss, animals would catch her scent, and finish her off.

As for the rest of the teachers and students, the parasite and its allies could have them.

Wait, I'm supposed to be protecting people and fighting for them, not hoping that the parasite kills them!

A ripple of fear coursed through Jack at the thought of how easily the violent urges entered his mind. He hated Trent, Ms. Kurbik, and Ashley, but not to the point of mutilation and murder, especially when the price was nothing more than a sick satisfaction at their bloody ends.

Confused by his emotions, Jack dismissed these violent thoughts. As he walked into the dining hall, he noticed that most others had not arrived yet. Jack did not see anyone he had previously met or recognized, so he decided to sit next to a man who was sitting by himself. Jack knew what it felt like to sit alone, having no one to talk to; he did not want this man to endure the same. The man looked to be about in his late twenties. He was average height and weight, wore glasses perched upon a crooked nose, had a neatly trimmed, black goatee, and closely cropped black hair.

Jack sat down next to him and said as casually as he could, "Hey, what's up?"

The man did not reply in any way, in fact he stayed in the same position without moving. Feeling that he had said something wrong, Jack decided it would be appropriate to perhaps introduce himself.

"I'm Jack, Jack Clark," said Jack enthusiastically, extending his hand for the man to shake.

The man did not shake Jack's hand nor introduce himself.

"Sir, have I said something to offend you or do you just not want me to sit here, because I'll move if you want me to. I'm just trying to make conversation. I'm new to Walkrins, so I'm just trying to meet people, getting to know this place, you know what I mean?"

The man finally turned his head in Jack's direction. "You're a prick," he muttered.

He abruptly stood up, glared at Jack for a moment longer, and then briskly walked out of the dining hall without eating.

Soon after the man left the dining hall, Jack spotted Tony walking toward him. Tony's right eye was not only covered with bandages, but it was also covered with an eye patch. Guilt surged through Jack as he looked at Tony's eye, reminding him of the responsibility he held for the elderly man's predicament.

"Argh! Hello matey, I'm Captain Tony, and the most fearsome pirate the world 'as ever seen!" Tony chuckled as he seated himself beside Jack.

"Hey, Tony, I saw there was a guy sitting here earlier with a black goatee and glasses. Do you know who he is?"

"Oh sure, that's Justin Bryant. Why do ya ask?"

"I introduced myself to him and he responded by telling me I was a prick."

Tony grimaced. "I'm sorry to hear that. Don't be too offended, Justin can be very blunt about how he feels."

"What do you know about him?"

"Not much. We've only talked once or twice. He seems pretty quiet and usually keeps to himself. He doesn't like to talk much, and when he does, he gets straight to the point. Only other thing I know is that he was here long before me."

Tony paused as Ricardo placed a bowl of egg salad on their table. "Argh, matey, this ain't proper pirate food!"

Jack smiled, glad to have Tony sitting beside him. The rest of the meal was spent talking of less heavy matters such as sports and food. They were both so focused on their conversation that Jack did not realize what time it was.

He looked up at the clock and said, "I just realized, Tony, I gotta go to the Fighting Complex to learn swordplay from Rax. I'll see ya later."

Tony bid Jack farewell as he ran off to the Fighting Complex. As Jack entered, he saw that it was much more crowded than the last time he had been inside. Where there had been no one the previous night, there were about thirty people who were firing their guns at different targets. Among those who were aiming at the targets was Fred, who seemed to be doing better than anyone else. There were a few pairs of people who were sparring, and in the corner was Robert Rax who seemed to be fighting an imaginary enemy. Jack tried to keep his distance as he got close.

"Hi, I'm here to learn swordplay from you," said Jack rather quickly. If Jack was not good at swordplay, it would create doubt among members of Walkrins. They might not think that he was the only one who could destroy the parasite if they discovered he was a weak swordsman, and the fact that his father was "quite the swordsman" didn't help either.

Rax turned around, looking just as solemn as he had the previous night. "You are right on time. I like that. Precision is essential to swordplay."

"Are we going to be using real swords?" asked Jack, eying Rax's sword.

"Of course not, we'd kill each other if we did. We'll be using these wooden swords; they are the most effective means of practicing. I will give you a real sword once you have shown me that you are mature enough, and deserving, to wield one. Go over to those barrels and bins and pick out one of those wooden swords so we can begin."

Jack picked out a wooden sword that seemed somewhat well balanced in his hands and walked back over to Rax.

"Now, the simplest way to begin is to learn the different moves of parrying, guarding, and striking. Parrying and guarding are your defensive moves, to protect yourself from your opponent. Striking is your offensive moves, to attack your opponent. Most people believe that striking is most important, but you need to be effective in both ways. We'll start off with the basic moves of parrying. Watch me and then you'll try. Parry one, parry two, parry three, parry four, parry five, parry five A, parry six, guard. Parry seven, parry eight, guard. Now you try."

Jack gripped his sword and began to try repeating the steps of parrying Rax had just shown him. He did one and two correctly but messed up after that. "Watch me." The tone of Rax's voice stayed impassive, and his expression remained solemn. It took Jack several more tries, but he was eventually able to do the parrying moves with only a minor mistake here and there. "Good," said Rax, nodding his approval. "Now I will show you the guarding moves, the other defensive tactics."

Jack was able to master these moves much quicker than the parrying ones. "Very good," said Rax as he scratched his clean-shaven face. "And finally, your offensive strategy, the striking moves." These turned out to be the most complex moves yet. Jack thought it was merely jabbing and thrusting his sword forward, but it was far more difficult than that. It took him far longer to understand the attack moves than the parrying and guarding.

"You must be perfect," said Rax who circled around Jack as he watched him attempt the striking moves. "When you attempt to strike your opponent, you are lowering your defenses, and giving them an opportunity to attack you. You must only attack at the opportune moment, when you are positive you can either defeat your opponent, or damage them in some way." Jack tried to concentrate as hard as he could on perfecting his strikes, yet there were several of them he just could not master. "Imagine that you are attacking someone. Think of someone you hate, someone you would feel no remorse for injuring or killing."

Jack's first thought was of Trent, but then he realized there was someone he hated more than the bully. Jack imagined that Tom, the man who killed his father, Grassemer, and many others was standing before him. To Jack's surprise, he found that he was doing far better now that he believed he was using these attacks on Tom. He could almost see Tom standing before him, as calm and deadly as when he fought and killed Grassemer. Jack slew his enemy with each strike, from cleaving him in two to thrusting the wooden sword through his heart.

"Excellent, excellent, you have improved dramatically," said Rax. Jack could hear a sort of happiness in Rax's voice, which Jack hoped came from his improvement with the striking moves. However, Rax's expression remained impassive. "We do not have much time left, so I will teach you the different stances which you will take before you fight. Then you may leave."

Jack looked up at the clock and was surprised to see there was only ten minutes left in his lesson. Rax showed Jack the right stance, the left stance, the middle stance, the unicorn stance, and the rear woman stance. The unicorn stance was to lift the sword above the head with two hands. The rear woman stance was to bend down to either the left or right, and grasp the sword with both hands. Rax explained that the rear woman stance was mainly used with a double sided sword which had two blades and a hilt adjoining both sides. This would enable someone to defend and attack themselves from enemies coming in both directions. "It can also be used with a one sided sword, but it is harder and riskier because you have to hold your sword by the middle of the blade and you would cut your hand. Also, one of your sides is just the handle, whereas the other side is your blade. This creates a mismatch for you, and obviously your enemies will try to attack you from your weaker side with the sword handle."

With that, Jack's first sword lesson concluded. "Thank you, Rax, the lesson was awesome, I really enjoyed it." Rax nodded at Jack's compliment, and walked over to retrieve his real sword.

As Jack began to walk away, a sudden question popped into his mind. He burst out, "What was it like learning swordplay from my father? I heard that he taught you." Rax did not respond immediately, he stared at his sword as he ran his thumb across the flat of the blade.

"Your father was a good teacher."

Rax made no other comment and began to swing his sword, reengaging his duel with the imaginary enemy. Jack had expected a more detailed answer, but he supposed he would ask Rax about it another time, when he knew him better.

As Jack began to depart from the Fighting Complex a voice behind him said, "Hey kid, what do you think you're doing?" Jack whipped around and saw that Fred was standing there, a machine gun slung over his shoulder, a grin on his face.

"I just wanted to get your attention. Dinner's in about a half hour, so I'm gonna go put my gun back in my room and then do you wanna go eat?"

"Sounds good," said Jack, realizing he was quite hungry. He hadn't been real crazy about the egg salad at lunch. Jack followed Fred to his room, which was a good walk from the Fighting Complex.

"So how was your first lesson with Rax?" asked Fred.

"I liked it a lot. He taught me the parrying, guarding, and striking moves in addition to the different stances. Rax is a good teacher, but he seems kind of..." Jack tried to find the right word. Odd didn't seem to fit.

"Rax is different, that's what he is. He's an uncommonly good swordsman; it's a comfort to know that he's on our side." If there was one thing that made sense about Rax, it was that he was an incredible swordsman and Jack had to agree with Fred, it was good that Rax was not an enemy of Walkrins.

When they reached Fred's room, Jack was surprised that he knocked on the door.

"Don't you have your own room?" asked Jack.

"Nah, I share with Rachel. It's nice to have the company."

"Come in," called Rachel from inside the room. Fred pushed open the door and Jack walked in. As Jack entered he saw that Fred's room was not as nice as his, some of the paint was peeling off the wall, but he supposed this was to be expected, Fred had lived here his whole life. However, Fred's room was far larger, most likely due to the fact that it housed two people. Sitting in the middle of the room on a queen size bed, reading a book, was Rachel. She wore a white tank top and jean shorts, exposing her hairless, smooth arms and legs.

"Jack, nice to see you," said Rachel enthusiastically as she looked up from her book.

Jack tried to make some intelligent response but all that came out of his mouth was a squeaky sounding "Hi."

"Did Fred bring you here so he could show you our lovely walls?" asked Rachel as she closed her book. Jack was so mesmerized by Rachel, her long honey blonde hair, her smooth face, her perfect looking body, that he couldn't seem to make any type of response.

Luckily, he was saved by Fred. "I caught up with Jack as I was leaving the Fighting Complex, and I wanted to put my gun back in the room before we go to dinner."

"Let me go wash up first," said Rachel as she stood up from her bed.

"Are you all right, Jack? You look kind of funny."

"What?" said Jack, his thoughts still wrapped around Rachel.

"I said, are you okay? You look kind of pale."

"Oh, I'm fine," said Jack. After all three of them washed their hands, they headed down to dinner.

"So what were you doing in the Fighting Complex, Jack?" asked Rachel.

Determined to be himself, and not become enthralled by Rachel, Jack said perhaps too boisterously, "Rax was giving me sword fighting lessons."

"How'd you do?" asked Rachel.

"I did all right, but it wasn't like it was hard, I just did the parrying, guarding, and striking moves. He also showed me the different stances."

"That's exactly how Rax started me out on my first day of sword fighting," said Rachel with a small chuckle.

As they reached the dining hall, Jack was surprised to see that it was almost packed. At the very most, it had only been half full during lunch. Fred leaned over toward Jack and said, "It's always a lot more crowded from the start at dinner. I guess that's because it's usually the tastiest meal of the day and people want to make sure they get the freshest food."

With some difficulty, the three of them found an empty table in the corner of the dining hall. Jack saw many of the people he had already met as he looked around. Ryan and Tony were sitting several tables away, appearing to be in deep conversation as they both waved their hands animatedly. Golish was sitting next to his sumo wrestler bodyguards and Rax at the table farthest away. The sumo wrestler guards appeared to be falling off the chairs which were too small for their bodies. Rax was whispering something into Golish's ear, which Jack hoped Rax was about his first sword fighting lesson. Ricardo strolled in and out of the kitchen, carrying trays of steaming food. The only people who Jack had met who didn't seem to be at dinner were Justin and Sarah.

"Do either of you know where Sarah is?"

Fred shrugged, but Rachel leaned in closely, so close that her face was inches from Jack's. He felt a bizarre mix of excitement and fear as her face drew closer.

"I went to go see her because I'd heard she was back from her mission," whispered Rachel so quietly that only Jack and Fred could hear. "I went in and she was sobbing. I asked what was wrong but she wouldn't say. I think it's Grassemer, though."

"What?" muttered Fred who seemed surprised by the news. "She was never close to him."

"Can't she still be sad?" snapped Rachel.

"I suppose," murmured Fred. Then, under his breath, "But sobbing?"

"What are you three whispering about?"

Jack turned around and saw Ricardo who was standing behind Fred, holding a steaming tray of roasted chicken.

"Nothing important," said Fred who was eying the roasted chicken with a hungry look in his eyes as he licked his lips. "I didn't eat much for lunch, so could you put the chicken down?"

"It's not my fault you didn't eat a good lunch," grunted Ricardo as he lowered the chicken onto the table. "Blame Juan, he's the chief cook today. I'm only a server."

"I never said the food at lunch wasn't good, I just didn't eat much," said Fred who began loading chicken and fried rice onto his plate. Ricardo made an indistinguishable grunt and began walking back to the kitchen as he rubbed his beer belly. The meal was overall quiet; Fred and Rachel seemed content on eating in silence.

Jack had no problem with this. In the wake of silence, he formed an idea, an idea that might momentarily soothe him of his worries and troubles. Closing his eyes, blocking out all troubling thoughts, tuning out the chattering voices spread throughout the dining hall, Jack's attention turned to the tender texture of the roasted chicken, the tangy flavor of the added spices delighting his taste buds. Once done eating, Jack opened his eyes, the noises rushing back into his ears. He did not feel entirely at peace, but he did feel much calmer. It seemed that meditation in the simplest form could do wonders.

After finishing the meal, Fred finally broke the silence. "Is there anything you still want to see, Jack?"

Jack thought about it, envisioning everything he'd seen so far, recounting everything he'd been told. "The outside," he said at last. "I still haven't seen outside the hotel."

"Fred, you've been depriving our guest of the greatest thing we have to offer," said Rachel in an artificially critical tone.

"Let the deprivation not last a minute longer. Come on!"

The three of them stood up from their square table and exited the dining hall. They walked down the hallway that contained the basketball court, the exercise room, the Fighting Complex, and the library. They then walked through the marble entrance hall as Fred and Rachel began chattering with one another. As he walked, Jack turned around to look up at the upper floors, the uncanny feeling of being watched nagging at him. When Jack looked up, he found his instincts to be correct. On the sixth floor, Justin Bryant leaned against the black railing, staring down at Jack, his gaze unwavering. His intent stare was not what frightened Jack, it was the fact that he made no attempt to appear inconspicuous when Jack spotted him. Jack was about to shout up at him, when Fred tapped him on the shoulder. "Don't you want to see the outside?"

"Yeah," said Jack unconsciously. "But don't you see Justin staring down at us?"

"Who cares about Justin? He's a weirdo. Come on, we have better things to do."

Slowly, Jack turned around and walked toward the metal doors at the end of the marble entrance hall, Justin's gaze still bearing down on him. For a moment, Jack wondered how Grassemer would have dealt with such a situation. Part of Jack thought that Grassemer would not be bothered by someone staring down at him; another part thought that Grassemer would never dismiss even a minor incident without further consideration. But Grassemer was gone. Any answer Jack came up would be hypothetical. It was best to simply forget the incident.

111

When they reached the front entrance to the hotel, Jack found that neither Fred nor Rachel pushed the metal doors open. Instead, Fred knocked against both doors three times. They were then thrown open, revealing two men holding machine guns.

"We're going to walk around for a little bit," said Fred, directing his words at both men.

"Be back before the sun sets," both of them replied as they shuffled to the side.

Fred nodded and beckoned Rachel and Jack to follow. They stepped outside, and the men with the machine guns closed the metal doors behind them with a resounding thud. Jack's first impression of the outside was the overwhelming sight of greenness. Before them was a long and wide expanse of grass, unobstructed by any trees. Leaves were strewn about the grass, a light wind causing them to move about. The expanse of grass appeared to be the only open area; as far as Jack could see, everything else in sight was abundant with trees. He squinted in the distance, and was able to make out two boulders, horizontal of one another at the base of the trees. The sight of the boulders evoked memories of Grassemer's final moments, his desperate attempts to kill Tom with magic.

Disturbed by the memories triggered by the boulders, Jack turned away from the grass and the trees, facing his body toward the outside of the hotel. Just like most of the inside, the exterior of the hotel was made of concrete. Had Jack happened to stumble across the building, he would not have labeled it as a hotel judging from the outside. Jack had not realized it before, but the hotel had no windows. All the light was produced from fire and electricity. From his current viewpoint, it looked like a large block of concrete with metal doors carved into the bottom. Two men with machine guns were positioned in front of the doors, their weapons clutched in their hands, their eyes scanning the area before them. As he looked up, Jack spotted several men armed with sniper rifles perched on the rooftop. The number of firearms was unsettling, but Jack supposed it was necessary.

"How does Walkrins get all these weapons?" Jack muttered to Fred.

"We get them here and there," said Fred mysteriously. Jack waited for Fred to elaborate, but he did not. Jack merely hoped that the weapons were not obtained illegally. Then again, considering that many of their enemies were part of the government, it seemed unlikely that illegal transactions would be frowned upon.

Jack surveyed the hotel for a moment longer, thinking of when Grassemer said the hotel was nestled deep in the mountain. Multiple elevations of forest resided above the hotel. Being surrounded by trees and with the other elevations, Jack understood what Grassemer meant, why no one had ever found it before, why the hotel was hidden from the world.

The hotel may be hidden, but it's not inaccessible if people walk down the mountain, go to a nearby town or store for supplies, and then hike back up, thought Jack. *Besides, they can't be totally confident it's hidden if there are snipers on the rooftop and men guarding the front doors.*

"Are you ready to move on?" asked Fred.

Jack nodded and turned away from the hotel and the patch of grass, venturing into the thick nest of trees. Jack's footsteps padded against beds of soil and grass as he walked among the trees, the orange light of the setting sun bursting through the leaves, illuminating various sections of the mountain. The size and types of the trees differentiated. There were trees taller than the marble pillars inside the hotel and trees that weren't much taller than Fred or Rachel. The different types of trees were even greater, from mahogany, to chestnut, to oak, to maple, to cedar. Just as Jack began thinking how tranquil his current surroundings were, he was struck by a disturbing memory, the last time he'd been in a forest.

"There aren't Treegonts around here, are there?" asked Jack worriedly.

"As far as I know, no one has seen a Treegont in this area," said Fred.

"There's no need to worry," said Rachel gently, smiling at Jack. Jack looked back at Rachel and returned her smile with one of his own, the sight of her beautiful form and soft-spoken words putting his worries to rest. Jack's eyes stayed riveted on Rachel as he watched her elegant body stride among the trees. Worried that Fred may have caught him staring at his girlfriend, Jack hastily glanced away and followed Rachel while attempting to nonchalantly glance at her body.

After walking for several more minutes, Rachel stopped in front of a small meadow of dandelions. She stooped down and plucked one of the dandelions out of the field, her eyes transfixed on the flower just as mesmerizingly as Jack's eyes had been transfixed on her. Rachel stayed still, continuing to observe the dandelion until Fred slowly walked toward her, curving his arms around her waist. At Fred's touch, she leaned her head back, smiling lovingly up at her boyfriend, and placed the dandelion behind his ear. Fred smiled down at her, a smile that somehow seemed more genuine than any of the times he smiled at Jack.

Then, Fred lowered his head, and kissed Rachel on the mouth.

The instant their lips made contact, a boiling anger erupted within

Jack. Part of him knew the anger was nonsensical. Fred and Rachel were engaged in a romantic relationship. There was no reason why they shouldn't kiss one another. Yet Jack somehow felt betrayed, hurt, and envious. Was it because he wanted to be the one kissing Rachel? Maybe it was the fact that they could kiss each other anywhere, but had chosen to do so in front of Jack. It was as if both of them, Fred in particular, wanted to prove how deep their love was for one another, that no one, not even Jack with his supposed destiny, could break their love.

Slowly, Fred and Rachel broke apart from one another until both of their tall, attractive forms stood upright.

"The sun's almost set," said Fred, nothing in his tone suggesting that anything had just happened. "Let's head back to base."

Fred took the lead this time as Jack and Rachel followed him through the trees, the dandelion still sticking behind his ear. Along the way, the impulse to summon something natural continually nagged at Jack. His magical powers might be what it took to win Rachel's heart, yet Jack resisted. The truth was, Fred had been kind and helpful to Jack so far, showing him around the base, introducing him to members, sharing information. Whether or not Fred's actions by the dandelion meadow resulted out of a need to prove Rachel's love for him, Jack was convinced they loved and cared for one another. Attempting to win Rachel's love would only trigger negative feelings. Besides, there could be far greater repercussions; there was no telling how other Walkrins' members would react. It seemed that the best course of action to take was to treat Fred and Rachel as friends. Friendship was more than acceptable when considering that before Grassemer entered his life, Jack had had no friends.

The three of them reached the expanse of grass in front of the hotel which was barely visible from the lack of sunlight in the sky.

"You got back just in time," said one of the men with a machine gun as he opened the metal doors, allowing the three of them to reenter the hotel. Once inside, the doors slammed behind them with a loud clang. They walked across the marble entrance hall to the dining hall which was now empty, and up the flight of stairs. Fred and Rachel did not walk up with Jack to his room on the fifth floor. They stopped in front of the door leading to the fourth floor, the floor where their room resided.

Jack was about to tell both of them to have a good night, until Fred spoke up. "Tomorrow I'm on guard duty until six, so I won't see you until dinner."

"What's guard duty?" asked Jack.

"On guard duty you either guard the front entrance to the hotel or you go up on the roof, just like the guys we saw outside. If you're not stationed on the roof or at the front entrance, you can be the monitor in the camera room. You may not have noticed," Fred laughed and pointed to the ceiling where a soulless black lens gazed down at them, "but this place is loaded with cameras so we know what's going on at all times. I thought the cameras might have caught the spy on tape, but they haven't yet. I'll see you tomorrow, Jack. Have a good night."

"Good night," said Jack as he watched Fred and Rachel open the door and disappear out of sight onto the fourth floor. He remained motionless, his eyes still hovering on the spot where Fred and Rachel had been just a moment before, the two people he now knew he wanted as friends, not as enemies or lovers.

CHAPTER 20

That night, Jack was not only haunted by memories of Grassemer's death, but of the two men who had pursued him in both the cornfield and in the field where they died. Visions of their mangled corpses lying in pools of blood swam before Jack's eyes, threatening to make him sick. Jack rose from his bed several times and hurried to the bathroom, leaning over the toilet, vomiting the roasted chicken and fried rice from dinner. After retching, Jack stumbled back into his bed, his head spinning with sickening memories of death. This process ensued for the duration of the night until he finally dozed off.

When Jack woke up, he found he was about to fall out of bed. Groggily, he moved his body back to the center of the bed to prevent himself from falling onto the floor. Before going back to sleep, Jack glanced at the digital alarm clock perched on his nightstand, wanting to see how much time he had before he had to be at the Fighting Complex. It was one o'clock.

Realizing that he had to be at the Fighting Complex in an hour, Jack bolted out of bed and began to get dressed. He brushed his teeth as fast as he could, took a quick shower, and opened the door of his room, sprinting down the hallway, down the flight of stairs, and into the dining hall. Jack did not even bother to sit down; he merely grabbed two slices of pizza and shoved them into his mouth, wolfing them down as fast as possible, as if he was a competitive eater, giving no thought to the food he vomited during the night.

He then ran toward the Fighting Complex, threw open the metal doors and burst inside. It was not as crowded as the previous day, there was only one pair sparring, and only Tony was firing at the shooting targets. Jack supposed it was pretty hard getting used to firing a gun with only one eye. In the corner, in his usual spot, was Rax, who appeared to be fighting an imaginary enemy. He had been doing the same thing when Jack had entered the previous day. When Jack came closer, Rax turned around, looked at Jack and said, "You're early, two minutes early."

"It's better than being late, right?" said Jack.

"Not necessarily," said Rax, shaking his shaved head. "It is best to be right on time, to be precise. If you attempt to strike your opponent prematurely, it may be your fatal mistake." Jack was astounded that Rax was comparing sword fighting to his punctuality.

"I don't see much correlation between the two things, but whatever," said Jack with a shrug as he retrieved a wooden sword from the barrel and walked back over to Rax.

Three hours later, Jack emerged from the Fighting Complex, sweat dripping from his face, his brain whirring. Rax had made the lesson much harder. The parrying, guarding, and striking moves were only the very beginning, the building blocks to swordplay.

Jack walked over to the dining hall and spotted Rachel sitting with Sarah. He went over and sat down next to both of them, determined to treat Rachel as a friend. "Hi, Rachel, Sarah, how are both of you?" said Jack as he sat down.

"I'm doing all right," said Sarah. "I'm sorry I only got to briefly speak with you yesterday, I was just so distraught after finding out about Grassemer. He always seemed so invincible; he'd done so much to defy the parasite that a part of me thought he would never die."

Jack realized that part of him felt the same way, the fact Grassemer had survived so long had also made Jack believe that his mentor had been indestructible. Even his lies appeared indestructible; no one seemed to doubt Jack's supposed destiny. Despite all the lies, Jack was beginning to fully realize how thankful he was to have known him, to have learned from him. Even though he knew it was silly, Jack glanced around the dining hall, looking for Grassemer. No one even looked remotely like Grassemer, but there was a chance most of the people in the dining hall were only part of Walkrins because of Jack's mentor. Then, Jack realized there was someone else who wasn't in the dining hall, someone who should be there.

"Where's Fred?" asked Jack.

"He's on guard duty," said Rachel. "He's been on it since six in the morning. He should be here soon."

Jack felt as if he was in a dream; he could not possibly be sitting next to two of the most beautiful looking women in the world. At school no one had sat with him at lunch. No one had even talked to him unless it was for bullying purposes. Now, he sat beside two tall, gorgeous women, who actually spoke to him voluntarily.

Wanting to continue the conversation, but not knowing what to say to Rachel, Jack asked Sarah, "So what were you doing in Washington D.C.?"

"How'd you know I was in D.C.?" asked Sarah in a taken aback voice as she brushed her bangs out of her face.

"I saw in a—" Jack hesitated, wondering if he would sound whimsical and maybe even deranged if he claimed he saw her in a dream. Surely she knew about the magicians if she was part of Walkrins, but she might not be privy to the facts of magician dreams. Better to lie and play it safe than sound odd, especially when he wanted to get off on the right foot with Sarah who he had been fancifully thinking about ever since his dream. "Golish told me you went to the Lincoln Memorial, but he didn't tell me anything else," said Jack.

"I'm surprised Golish told you where I was because the nature of the mission was supposed to be a secret," said Sarah. "But I shouldn't be surprised. Golish can be so erratic."

Thank you Golish, thought Jack, thinking that Golish had saved him yet again, this time unknowingly.

Turning in Rachel's direction, he saw that she had a worried expression on her face, and kept glancing around the dining hall. Jack's first thought was she was looking to see if any food had come out; she was probably hungry. But then, Jack thought it was more likely that she was looking for Fred. She was probably worried that he had not come back from guard duty yet.

Looking at both women on either side, sexual fantasies began to erupt in his mind. He imagined he was in the middle of a barren desert with Sarah and Rachel. Terrified by their current surroundings, they pleaded for Jack to console them. He stripped off their clothes, rolling back in forth between both of them on the coarse sand as he passionately kissed them on the mouth, his hands groping their smooth skin, the sleek hair running down their backs. As he left each one, the other begged for him to come back, yearning to feel the lips of Jack Clark, their mighty savior, their protector, their—

"Can you move over just a bit, Jack?"

Jack snapped back to reality at the sounds of these words, causing the tantalizing thoughts to evaporate.

"Oh, Fred," said Rachel in a relieved voice, "I was beginning to worry."

"About what?" said Fred as Jack moved over, giving Fred more legroom.

"Well you've been on guard duty so long and I just wondered..." Rachel trailed off with a semi-embarrassed look on her face.

"Don't worry, Rachel, I'm fine and I'm here." Fred said this in a matter-of-fact way, but Jack thought he saw a pleased look flit across Fred's face.

Ricardo, Juan, and the other cooks brought out dinner, which happened to be pizza and salad, the same as lunch.

"This is the same food they served at lunch," complained Jack.

"With so many people, and the fact we live in the mountains, the cooks can only make so much food," said Fred who grabbed a slice of pizza as soon as it was put down on the table. He gobbled up the pizza in one bite as he rolled the slice up and shoved it whole into his mouth.

"Fred, I've told you, don't eat so fast, you're going to choke some day if you keep doing that," said Rachel who seemed half skeptical, half amused at the way Fred practically inhaled the slice of pizza.

"Sorry, I was feeling lightheaded; I had to get some food." Fred began to drown his salad in a pool of Italian dressing. Jack laughed as he watched Fred, thinking that his mother would like Fred quite a lot. She loved pouring condiments and different sauces on her foods, especially different types of chocolate sauces on desserts.

As Jack thought about this he realized how much he missed her. Before he had met Grassemer, and had come to Walkrins, she had been the only one who had cared about him. His mother had cared about him before everyone thought he was going to be a hero, before he had magical powers. Susan Clark had loved her son for who he was, not because of what he might become.

"I can't figure out how you eat so much Fred," said Sarah, her voice bringing Jack out of his thoughts. "I wish I could eat like you, I really love food, but I couldn't bear being fat."

"I don't know, I guess I exercise a lot. My mother was the same way, she would eat a ton, but she was always skinny." Fred grabbed yet another slice of pizza as he finished speaking.

"Speaking of that, we need to do some exercise tonight, to work off this pizza," said Rachel.

"How about basketball?" said Fred.

"Sounds good," said Jack.

"I'm in," said Sarah.

"Great, basketball wins. Let's allow our food to settle and then go change."

The four of them went to their respective rooms to change, and then met at the basketball court. They didn't play any really competitive games; they just shot around, and played simple games such as knockout. It turned out that Fred was quite good at basketball; he made every single free throw during knockout. All of them were in a goofy mood, but no one was goofier than Sarah. She started speaking in an amusing accent which caused Jack, Fred, and Rachel to fall into laughing fits.

Sarah would make comments with her amusing accent like "yo, give me the rock here homies," and "yo, I got this fellas, I got this. I'm gonna dunk this basketball so hard, that I'm gonna shatter the backboard." Sarah jumped up and tried to dunk it, but despite the fact she was tall, the ball didn't even touch the rim. Fred gave a little snort. "Yo, you think you can do better Fred?" said Sarah, who was pretending to sound angry in her amusing accent, although she was struggling not to laugh.

Several hours later, after many more laughs and missed shots, Sarah, Jack, Fred, and Rachel trudged back to their rooms, somewhat tired from all the running around. As Jack lay in his bed, trying to fall asleep, he felt something, something he had never felt before. He could not explain the feeling, but he knew he had never felt this way, at least toward anyone close to his age. After some thought Jack realized it was a feeling of exhilaration and acceptance after spending enjoyable times with friends.

CHAPTER 21

As days turned into weeks at Walkrins, Jack unintentionally formed a daily routine. He continued to practice and have sword lessons with Rax everyday for three hours. Afterwards, he would go to the dining hall and eat dinner with the usual company of Fred, Rachel, and Sarah.

At dinner, he would always spy out Golish, go over to his table, and ask if his mother had called back.

"She hasn't called back yet, but I'm sure she's just busy, or hasn't checked her messages. Don't worry, Grassemer sent members of Walkrins to protect her in case she was attacked," said Golish when Jack asked for the first time. After the first day, Golish always replied to Jack's question with the same response. "No word from her, but I'm sure she'll call in the next day or so."

"Well, why don't you call one of the people Grassemer sent to protect her?" asked Jack one day, frustrated that Golish had not done the obvious yet.

"None of them have cell phones," said Golish. "I'm one of the only people here who has one, actually." Jack accepted that there was nothing else to do; he would simply have to wait for his mother's response, and hope she was all right.

After eating dinner with his companions and briefly talking to Golish, Jack would spend a good deal of the night with Fred, Rachel, and Sarah. Whether this was playing basketball, working out in the exercise room, reading in the library, or simply talking, Jack always enjoyed himself immensely.

Afterwards, Jack would return to his room, and struggle to fall asleep, memories of Grassemer's death consuming his mind. Eventually, exhaustion overcame terror, and he would fall asleep, waking up around noontime, which gave him time to eat lunch, and then he would learn swordplay from Rax at the Fighting Complex. Jack usually slept through breakfast, but he felt it was okay because he ate large portions at both lunch and dinner. Sleeping in, staying up late, training with Rax, and hanging out with Fred, Rachel, and Sarah became Jack's basic schedule.

To Jack's enormous relief, Sarah did not pester him about how he knew she was in Washington D.C. Jack also began noticing that many of the people he saw appeared uptight. They walked down the halls with weapons slung over their shoulders or belted to their waists, grim expressions dominating their features. Most would ignore Jack when he walked past them, but a few would give curt nods as they sped past him, intent on reaching their destinations. Not wanting to fraternize with these solemn folk, Jack tried to only spend time with Fred, Rachel, Sarah, Ryan, and Tony.

Fred and Tony were being assigned to guard duty almost daily, so Jack never ate lunch with either of them, but usually with Rachel and Ryan (Sarah was working in the library during lunch). Ryan revealed many details about his past during these meals, explaining to Jack that "I was going into the medical field, but I had to leave my career behind when it was discovered I was gay. Aside from Rachel, I'm really the only one here with medical experience, so I tend to anyone who is injured or sick, and when there's no one to treat, I create medicines and ointments. I have my own lab. Many of the medicines and ointments I've created are quite effective, and I could make lots of money off it, but Golish won't let me sell it. He says I'll be caught, sent to solitary confinement, the parasite will find out I'm part of Walkrins, and it'll make me give away our whereabouts. What does it matter anyway? They know where to find us. That's why Fred, Tony, Justin, and many others are on guard duty every day, Golish is nervous there's going to be an attack any day now."

During meals, Juan would sometimes wheel himself over toward Jack and inform him that the cooks were low on certain fruits and vegetables. Jack responded by summoning whichever fruits and vegetables Juan asked for into a large crate.

Pleasantly surprised, Jack found that because he was exercising more frequently, he was losing weight. "So all these exercise rooms explain why I'm the fattest person here," said Jack with a small chuckle, taking a stab at himself while he pedaled on one of the exercise bikes.

"Exercise is the key to staying fit," said Rachel who was running on a treadmill.

"Exercise is good," agreed Sarah who was riding an exercise bike next to Jack.

As time wore on, Fred was joining their nightly activities less and less; Golish was continually assigning him to guard duty. Rachel stopped joining Jack and Sarah as frequently. Jack could tell she sorely missed Fred, who was more important to her than anything in the world.

Jack, however, did not mind the absence of Fred and Rachel; it allowed him to spend the evenings alone with Sarah, which often took place in the library. On their first evening there, while Sarah browsed the volumes on the bookshelves, she asked, "What's your favorite book genre?"

"I don't like to read, so I guess I don't have a favorite," said Jack.

"You don't like reading!" exclaimed Sarah as she whipped around, an astonished expression upon her beautiful face. "There's nothing more enjoyable than reading a good book. Read some of the classics and then you'll understand what I mean. Here, this book ought to get you hooked." She plucked a volume off the shelf and handed it to Jack. He examined the cover, seeing that it was *Fahrenheit 451*, by Ray Bradbury. Had anyone else given Jack a book to read, he probably wouldn't have gone through with it. But Jack wanted to please Sarah and spend as much time with her as possible. So, he plopped down into one of the red armchairs in the corner of the library and began reading. Sarah sat across from him, her face hidden by a book called *Jane Eyre*, by Charlotte Brontë. Jack planned to skim the book, and spend more of his time stealing glances at Sarah's attractive form. But as soon as he started *Fahrenheit 451*, he was as Sarah had predicted, hooked. He eagerly raced through the book, enthralled by the futuristic society woven by Ray Bradbury, amazed by the parallels it held to current day society.

As he read, he felt an increasing connection to the protagonist, Guy Montag. It was as if he and Montag were on a similar journey. Both had been content with their lives, yet they failed to see the purposelessness of it all. It was only when a single individual entered both of their lives that they began to question the world around them. In Montag's case it was the young girl Clarisse, and in Jack's case it was Grassemer. Jack only hoped that like Montag, he would be able to one day take a stand against injustice and fight back.

Before Jack knew it, he had finished the book. He stared at the concrete floor for a moment, the powerful images lingering with him.

He looked up and saw Sarah smiling at him. "Did you enjoy it?" she whispered.

"It was great," said Jack. "It's the best book I've ever read. Thank you so much."

Sarah laughed. "You may not feel the same way after you read some other books. But I'm glad you liked it. Bradbury is a wonderful writer. Now come on, it's past midnight, we should go to bed."

That night, Jack fell asleep much quicker than usual, thoughts of *Fahrenheit 451* managing to partially block out the bloody images that had haunted him for the past few nights. After *Fahrenheit 451*, Sarah introduced Jack to her favorite book and favorite play: *Jane Eyre* by Charlotte Brontë, and *Romeo and Juliet* by William Shakespeare. Through her two favorites, Jack gained a better understanding of the woman he fervently admired. Like Romeo and Juliet, Jack suspected she would sacrifice everything if she believed she found her true love. And like Jane Eyre, Jack believed that Sarah would only settle for love as long as she maintained her individuality and ability to utilize free will.

Not only did these stories give Jack a better understanding of Sarah, but they also helped him examine love and infatuation, the topic he had asked Grassemer about in the cornfield. Jack studied the relationship Jane Eyre had with Mr. Rochester, and Romeo with Juliet. Just like the parallels Jack saw between himself and Guy Montag in *Fahrenheit 451*, he saw parallels with his feelings and relationship with Sarah through her favorite book and play. Jack knew he was no Romeo who could pronounce his love through eloquent poetry, but he believed despite his lack of poetry skill, he loved Sarah as much as Romeo loved Juliet. His heart leapt whenever he saw her for the first time each day and his blood ran thick with excitement. Jack began telling himself that this feeling was pure love for Sarah, and he loved her for the person she truly was, not because of her looks. It was different than with Rachel, he had merely been fascinated by her attractiveness and the fact a female other than his mom spoke to him as an equal. Jack convinced himself he had been infatuated with Rachel, but he truly loved Sarah.

CHAPTER 22

One particular morning, Jack woke earlier than usual, his daily sword lesson with Rax still several hours away. With nothing to do, Jack made his way toward Sarah's room, hoping he could spend the morning with her before she began her librarian duties. He knocked on her door but there was no reply. Jack also went to Fred and Rachel's room, and knocked, but they did not reply either. Thinking about what else he could do, Jack decided that he would meet with Golish, to ask about his mother, and to also ask about his father, for Golish had expressed a desire to discuss Jack's father with him. Intrigued by the sudden opportunity to make this request come to fruition, Jack began making his way toward Golish's office. The two sumo wrestler bodyguards flanked the entrance to his office, their axes held aloft.

"Who goes there?" asked the guard on the left as Jack approached.

Remembering how Fred responded to this question, Jack declared, "It is I, Jack Clark, here to see Mr. Golish."

"You may enter," growled the guards in unison as they lowered their axes and opened the door.

Jack passed through the entrance and began walking down the hallway leading to Golish's office. As Jack peered inside, he spotted Golish sitting behind his untidy desk, typing into a laptop seated on his lap.

"Uh, Mr. Golish?" said Jack tentatively, announcing his presence.

Golish's head jerked upward at the sound of Jack's voice. For a moment he stared at Jack as if he did not recognize him, but the next moment his face split into a wide grin. "Jack, how nice of you to stop by." Then, Golish's expression sagged as it dawned on him why Jack was most likely in his office. "I'm sorry, she hasn't called back."

"That's not the only reason I'm here," said Jack quickly, trying to conceal his disappointment over Golish's last statement, eager to ask about his father.

"Well, sit down, then," said Golish, gesturing at the chair across from his desk.

Jack did as he was told, noticing that as he sat down that Golish wore the same wrinkled white t-shirt and plaid pajama pants that he had been wearing when Jack had first met him. His hair was just as untidy and his beard even scragglier than the last time Jack had seen him. Golish had made no effort to clean off his desk; it was still covered in jumbles of papers.

"So, tell me, Jack, apart from asking about your mother, why are you here?" asked Golish curiously as he stroked his scraggly beard.

"Well you told me that you'd like to talk about my father sometime, so I thought seeing as I woke up earlier than usual and I have nothing to do for a few hours that I'd take advantage of this time and talk with you about my dad."

"Ah, yes, Jason. Good man, good friend. Not a day goes by where I don't think of him."

Golish turned his laptop around and pointed at the screen. "You see that there? Those four young people? That's me, with your father, and Ben and Jessica Waxston, Fred's parents. This photo was taken by Grassemer shortly after we met at this hotel. Four young people, ready to make our marks on the world."

Jack's eyes fell on his father as he examined the picture. Jason Clark had a clean-shaven face, was medium height and weight, and had short black hair. Jack's face was radically different from his father; Jason's face was not chubby and layered with pimples. A bright grin lit up his handsome face, his arm wrapped around a man who looked identical to Fred Waxston. Jack assumed the man was Fred's father, Ben, who beamed at the camera, happy to be amongst his friends. Standing next to Ben was a slender woman whose caramel colored hair was tied back in a ponytail. Although Fred looked most like his father, he also bore a slight resemblance to his mother. As Jack's eyes flitted to the next man in the photo, his jaw nearly dropped open in shock.

It was Golish, but a much younger version with a beard barely visible on his chin, his hair combed. He wore a polo shirt which was tucked into beige dress pants. Golish's drastically different appearance caught Jack off guard, it was only the deep bags under his eyelids and a similar face that was not yet wrinkled that enabled Jack to identify the younger version of the Walkrins' leader.

"It's a nice picture," said Jack as he pushed the laptop back toward Golish.

"I'm glad you think so. You know, on days where I feel as if I don't give a damn anymore, this is what I look at. My three friends give me hope. They died in the course of duty. I refuse to have let them died in vain."

Golish paused, leaned back in his chair, and began mumbling words as if almost to himself. "There we are all in that picture, determined to change the world for the better. And now they're all gone."

"What about Fred's father? Isn't he a Joinx?

Golish grunted. "Ben's worse than dead. He's nothing more than a pawn that doesn't know shit other than the parasite's orders. He could kill Fred and not have a clue that it's his son. The moment that needle was injected, Ben Waxston perished. All that's left now is a man whose entire identity has been obliterated, his entire being consumed by the parasite. Those fine people, my three friends, are gone. Now only old and incompetent Golish is left."

"I don't think you're incompetent," ventured Jack, worried by the state of misery into which Golish seemed to be sinking.

At the sound of Jack's words, Golish seemed to come out of his trancelike condition. He leaned forward in his chair, still mumbling. "I fear you are mistaken. I am unfortunately quite incompetent. I cannot run this organization without the help of my three friends and Grassemer. You don't believe me? Here, I will show you something that will illustrate the truth."

Golish snatched the laptop off his desk and began tapping away at the keys with an unnecessary amount of force. He then spun it around and shoved it at Jack. "Look at these documents. Endless lists, records, and data. The name of every member that has ever been a part of this organization, including the day they joined and the day they left or died if that information applies to them. Every battle we ever fought, blueprints of every plan, every weapon purchase, the daily budget. The date of every press conference or television appearance that the parasite has made through the body of Brandon Jones. Every single newspaper article or other news tidbit that deals with the parasite and anything connected to it. Now look more closely at these documents. Do you see changes for the worse in these past few weeks? You see how low our daily budget has been for quite some time, that we are short on weapons? Did you know that you're the only new member we've had since that Eddie fellow joined four months ago? Now ponder on all of that, and still look me in the eye and tell me that I'm not incompetent."

Golish slammed the laptop shut and shoved it to the side of his untidy desk. He breathed heavily for a few moments and then his head flopped onto his desk. A moan escaped his lips as he clawed at individual papers, not bothering to check if they were documents of importance. Jack watched Golish for a whole five minutes, entranced by his bizarre behavior. Finally, Golish lifted his head, sank back into his chair, his hands shaking slightly. "I'm sorry," he gasped. "I'm just overwhelmed by all this responsibility. I had no right to lash out at you like that."

"It's all right, Mr. Golish, I understand."

"I'm just sick of this war. With my friends gone I can't even find a source of enjoyment anymore. It's frustrating to see others enjoying themselves and never doing any honest work when I'm loaded down with responsibility. Some of these folks can't even fight, I mean, truth be told, they're practically useless. Don't worry, I'm not referring to you, Jack. You've been great for Walkrins. You've given the people hope, and Rax tells me you are becoming an excellent swordsman."

"I don't know about that," said Jack sheepishly.

"There's no need to be so modest. I would expect nothing less than excellence from the son of Jason Clark. Now, I really do appreciate you stopping by, but I must return to my work." Golish stood up, shook Jack's hand, and returned to his desk.

When Jack walked to the door, he noticed a spider dangling from the ceiling by a string of web. As it lowered itself, the spider disconnected from the web and plummeted to the ground.

CHAPTER 23

Several days after his meeting with Golish, Jack headed to the Fighting Complex, ready to receive the sword that Rax had promised to give him. Jack threw open the metal doors, expecting to see Rax holding a polished sword. However, Rax was nowhere to be seen; in fact only one person stood in the whole Fighting Complex which was odd for the afternoon. Standing in Rax's usual corner, was Sarah, who looked up at Jack with an exuberant smile. She wore a plain white t-shirt and blue gym shorts, yet she still looked stunningly beautiful.

"Sarah," said Jack in surprise, "what are you doing here? Where's Rax?"

"He's on guard duty. More than half of Walkrins is on guard duty because people are leaving the base for the first time since you showed up."

"Why?"

"Ryan and Ricardo took the helicopter, stationed it several miles from a nearby town, and are getting food and medical supplies. Some members on guard duty are moving around the town, disguised in case either Ricardo or Ryan are attacked. If those who are disguised are in danger, more members of Walkrins will come and help. Rax volunteered to be one of the disguised because he's one of the best fighters in Walkrins."

Jack had initially felt disappointed that Rax was not in the Fighting Complex, ready to give Jack his real sword. However, seeing Sarah seemed to evaporate his initial disappointment. "So what are you going to teach me?" asked Jack.

"Oh, I don't think you need any more training. We'll just spar, one on one, and we'll see who is better. After sparring we'll go to dinner, and after dinner I have a surprise for you. Sound good?"

"Yep," said Jack, intrigued by the surprise awaiting him after dinner. Concerning sparring, he had never seen Sarah fight before, he was unsure of how adept she was with a sword. Initially, they circled around one another, their wooden swords raised, daring the other to strike first. After a while, Jack became tired of the constant circling, and began to lose his focus. Sarah took advantage of his momentary lapse of concentration and she stabbed him in his left hip, which would have been far more painful in a real battle.

"Even after all those times Rax told you to keep your guard up, focus solely on your opponent, you still let that happen," said Sarah as both of their wooden swords collided in midair. "He taught me as well Jack," she winked, "and I do have more experience."

"That shouldn't be a problem," chuckled Jack who attempted to thrust his sword at Sarah's leg, but she reacted perfectly and parried his blow. At first, Jack didn't want to go too hard on Sarah, but she was not restraining against him. As her sword slashed across his stomach, Jack decided to fight to the best of his abilities. He began attacking her from all angles, and her attacks were striking him less and less. Their defenses became so good that eventually neither of them could get a strike past each other.

"Stop," said Sarah whose forehead was covered in beads of sweat.

"We're quite even," said Jack as he stowed his wooden sword back in the barrel.

"Yes, maybe that's why I like you so much," said Sarah quietly. Jack waited for her to elaborate, for Sarah to express her undying love for him, but she said nothing on that matter. "Want to go have dinner?" asked Sarah, gesturing to the doorway of the Fighting Complex, leading to the dining hall.

"Sure," replied Jack, his stomach rumbling faintly as he walked to the door with Sarah at his side.

When they reached the dining hall, Jack noticed it was practically empty. In fact, Jack did not recognize anybody in the whole dining hall except for Juan who was wheeling toward Jack and Sarah with a tray of gyros.

"Hi, Jack, hi, Sarah," said Juan. "You don't have any news on what is happening with Ricardo, do you?"

"I'm sorry, Juan," said Sarah in an apologetic voice. "I've been working in the library and sparring with Jack all day, I wouldn't know."

"It seems as if everyone is on guard duty, or on that blasted mission except us," complained Juan. "My brother and Ryan are out there getting supplies; Rax and Justin are in the town, disguised. Fred, Rachel, Tony, and Golish are here, but they're listening in on what's going on."

Jack personally did not care that he was not part of the mission because it allowed him to spend the evening alone with Sarah. After eating, Sarah suggested that they both head back to their rooms and change into a fresh set of clothes, and then meet each other back in the Fighting Complex where Jack's surprise would be held.

"The surprise doesn't involve fighting. It's just that all the open space in there makes the surprise more beneficial." She winked at Jack, stood up from the table, and walked out of the dining hall.

After changing into clean clothes, Jack headed to the destination of Sarah's surprise. He did not pass a single person on his way to the Fighting Complex. It appeared that the majority of Walkrins was still absorbed with the mission to acquire food and medical supplies. Shortly after setting out from his room, Jack found himself standing in front of the identical metal doors leading to the Fighting Complex. Feeling mainly excited but also somewhat nervous, Jack took a deep breath, and pushed his hands against the metal doors.

As Jack stepped inside, his eyes immediately landed on the lone person standing in the center of the complex. Entranced, Jack gazed at Sarah, her seemingly perfect form clad in a strapless, white dress, radiating an opulent, yet pure beauty. She began walking toward Jack, a smile lighting up her flawless face, her long black hair falling against her shoulders. She walked toward Jack in a graceful manner, striding in what almost seemed like slow motion, giving the situation a surreal feeling. Sarah stopped several feet in front of Jack, staring into his eyes, still smiling broadly. Disregarding any feeling of awkwardness, Jack continued to stare at her, determined to drink in every aspect of her elegant beauty.

"Hey," said Sarah, suddenly breaking the silence between them as well as the staring.

"Hey. I'm uh, um..." Jack trailed off, shaking his head in attempt to not become tongue-tied. "I'm sorry I didn't get dressed up."

"You weren't supposed to. This is a surprise for you." Sarah turned away from Jack and walked over to a corner of the Fighting Complex. She then whipped around and asked, "Do you like music?"

"I'm not much of a music person, but I guess I like it."

"Music is one of the few beauties left in the world," said Sarah mysteriously. She bent down, picked up a boom box, and pressed several buttons. As Sarah walked back to where Jack was standing stiff as a statue, a voice emitted out of the boom box, a woman singing a song Jack had never heard before.

"Do you dance, Jack?"

"Not at all," said Jack, somewhat sheepishly.

"There's no reason to sound so ashamed about it," said Sarah sweetly. "Dancing is another one of the few true beauties that exist. The world was once a place full of wondrous beauties. Sadly, few of them remain. Over time evil has spread and destroyed these purities. We must ensure that the few that linger will endure. I asked you to come here tonight, Jack, so I could share two of the few beauties that remain. Tonight, we will dance to good music. I even decided to get dressed up for the occasion in an attempt to add more beauty to the occasion, but I don't know if I look any better."

"You're always beautiful," said Jack, "but you're especially gorgeous tonight."

"You're too kind," chuckled Sarah as she brushed her bangs out of her eyes.

"No, I'm not. If there is any beauty that I'm sure exists, it's you, in every possible way I person can be beautiful."

Sarah gracefully strode toward Jack and gently placed one hand on his shoulder, and clasped his other hand. Jack's empty hand dangled at his side, unsure of what to do with it until Sarah picked it up, and curled it around her waist. Then, without a slight moment of hesitation, they began dancing. They started out fast, but as time progressed they slowed down the tempo. The movements were awkward, Jack moved clumsily, stepping on Sarah's bare feet several times which caused him to break into endless apologies. Sarah did not seem to care about Jack's inelegant dancing abilities. She would simply smile at him and whisper in an endearing voice that it was perfectly all right. Jack eventually kicked off his sneakers as he continued to dance with Sarah. They were mostly silent, the only noise in the Fighting Complex being their movement and the songs emanating from the boom box. Tall as she was, Jack found himself gazing up at Sarah, a tender smile etched across her face. Jack had never been so close to Sarah before, her face appearing to be even more striking up close.

At one point, Jack rested his head against Sarah's bare chest, his head slightly raised above her firm breasts. He closed his eyes, his pimply cheek lying against her smooth skin. Sarah relinquished her grasp on Jack's shoulder and began gently running her fingers through Jack's short black hair. She then moved her hand to Jack's cheek which she began to caress, her fingers brushing against his pimples. Normally this would have hurt, but Jack's focus was directed on the soft texture of her hand, her loving gesture.

Suddenly filled with the impulse to confess his feelings for her and deciding that there would be no better time to do so, Jack began to rack his brains, trying to find the right words to express his feelings. Jack's thoughts were so consumed by formulating the wording of his assertion of love that he failed to realize the music had stopped playing. He was brought back to reality as Sarah withdrew her hand from Jack's cheek and whispered, "Good night, Jack." She smiled at him for a moment, then strode toward the metal doors, swung them open, and was gone. Disappointed that the evening had ended without his confession and Sarah's sudden departure, Jack trudged back to his room, wondering if he would ever be able to tell Sarah how he felt about her.

Chapter 24

Jack woke early the next day to discover that the mission to obtain the food and medical supplies had gone well, everyone was safe, and no one had been discovered.

"Golish reckons it went too well," Fred whispered to Jack as they sat at breakfast together. "He's paranoid, says it was all part of the spy's plan to let the mission work smoothly. Honestly, it was a waste of time to have all those guards. I mean, the parasite isn't going to care if we buy a few groceries, is it? If it's smart, it would attack when we're totally unprepared, not when we've got more than half of the organization ready to fight if necessary."

Jack was hardly listening to Fred; he still felt disappointed that his evening with Sarah had gone awry. He was glad to go to his sword fighting lesson with Rax; he wanted something to take his mind off last night's events.

"You're on time, Jack. Good, very good," said Rax as Jack entered the Fighting Complex.

Jack had forgotten about Rax's promise to give him a real sword, and his pangs of disappointment were replaced by excitement as Rax picked up a long sword, with a sharp tip, and monkeys carved around the hilt.

"Uh, why are there monkeys carved into the handle?" asked Jack who thought the design was amusing and a bit bizarre.

"Your father picked the design. This was his sword. It was retrieved after his death. As his son, it is rightfully yours."

Never in his life had Jack had any possession that his father had owned. Awed, Jack grasped the sword, his hand curved around the monkey engraved hilt. The sword was heavy; Jack felt that it would be far different than fighting with a wooden sword.

"Just swing it around, get used to it. I know it feels much heavier than the wooden swords, but we have to train with them. If we used real swords we would kill one another. After you feel somewhat comfortable with it, we will try the parrying moves with one another."

Three hours later, Jack left the Fighting Complex, his father's sword swinging from his belt in a black sheath. It was then and there that Jack made his decision. Time for hesitation was over, he needed to confront Sarah and see if she felt the same way about him. He scanned the dining hall but saw Sarah was not there.

"She's not working in the library," muttered Jack to himself, "so she must be in her room." He began running, sprinting up the stairs and down the hallway as fast as he could, while his father's sword swung at his side, somehow giving him confidence. Breathing heavily, Jack reached her door, and knocked, hoping she was inside.

"Come in," called Sarah's voice. Jack turned the knob of the door, his heart beating furiously. "Jack!" exclaimed Sarah as he entered the room. She lay under the covers of her bed in a pink t-shirt and plaid pajama pants; it looked as if she had been in bed all day. "Sorry I'm still in bed, I woke up a long time ago. I just wanted to lay here, relax, and let my mind wander. People always seem to be doing something, always heading some place. Sometimes it's good just to look around you, stop what you're doing. Sometimes you just have to slow down." Her last sentence came out as a whisper, in a somewhat tender sounding voice. Jack stared at her, mesmerized by her beauty, in her looks and as the person he thought she was. "Come and sit down on the bed with me," said Sarah. Jack sat down, trying to begin saying what he wanted to tell her. "So what's up, Jack?"

He took a deep breath, and began to speak. "Before I was involved with Walkrins, before I met Grassemer, before I left home, I had a dream. You see, those with magical water within them have dreams of events that are happening in the present, something that will affect them in some way. The first dream I ever had like this, was with you. I'm sorry, but I lied to you that night at dinner. I knew you were in Washington D.C. because I dreamt that you were at the Lincoln Memorial, not because Golish told me. In the dream, the three Joinxs came and you were trying to hide from them. But I didn't know whether or not you escaped because my mom woke me up.

"I worried for those two weeks I spent with Grassemer that you hadn't escaped and the Joinxs had caught you. Even though I had only seen you in a dream, I couldn't help but fall in love with you. You seemed so beautiful, so poised, and so brave. I couldn't stop thinking about you. When I met you in Golish's office, I felt so relieved that you were okay. I love you, Sarah, more than anything. I would rather die than lose you." Jack saw Sarah's eyes were full of tears, whether they were happy or sad, Jack did not know. He waited to hear her response.

After what seemed like an eternity of silence, as they sat on the bed together, Sarah whispered, "I love you too, Jack."

But it was not over. There was still something else Jack had to tell her. Grassemer had told Jack to tell no one, but if he couldn't trust Sarah with a secret, then he couldn't trust anyone.

"There is something else I need to tell you," said Jack, his hands beginning to shake because he was so nervous. "Everyone thinks that I'm the only one who can destroy the parasite, that I will end this war. But it is only a rumor, a rumor that Grassemer created. He did this to create fear among our enemies, and hope among our allies. Grassemer had no proof that I could destroy the parasite. Truthfully, you, or Fred, or Rax, or Rachel, or anyone else has just as good of a chance of destroying the parasite as me. I am telling you this for several reasons. Firstly, if we truly love one another, then we should always be honest with each other. Secondly, I need to know, do you still love me now that you know I'm not destined to destroy the parasite?"

Sarah stared at Jack, her expression unreadable. Then, she leaned forward so close that her lips were only an inch away from Jack. "I love you more than anything in the world, regardless of your future." She placed both her hands on Jack's cheeks as she bent forward, preparing to kiss him.

Then with a bang, Sarah's door was thrown open. As her door slammed into the wall, Sarah leapt away from Jack, so the person who opened the door would not see what had happened. Standing in the doorway, stroking his goatee with a sneer on his face, was Justin.

"You should have knocked, Justin," said Sarah rather lamely.

"Oh, why should I have done that? I would have missed all the fun."

"What do you mean?" said Sarah a bit too quickly.

"You were always a distinguished woman, Sarah, always respectable. I was repulsed to discover you spend your evenings with scum like this." He nodded his head in Jack's direction. "What happened, Sarah? How did he twist your intelligent mind?"

"He's quite the charmer," said Sarah, beaming at Jack.

Justin's eyes scanned Jack's face, resting for a moment on the enormous pimple perched on the edge of Jack's nose.

"Very charming," muttered Justin under his breath. "Anyway, I'm not here for you," said Justin, his voice rising as he nodded at Jack. "I came here to tell Sarah that Golish wants to see her. But you better come as well. Golish ought to know what the supposed hero is up to in his spare time."

"You can't make either of us go anywhere," said Jack, trying to sound brave, although it did not come out that way.

"Then I'll just tell Golish that you think you are superior to everyone else, you think he is beneath you, and you do not have time to see him."

"Jack, let's just go, we'll see Golish and then we'll be rid of Justin."

"Fine," said Jack, who only agreed because he would do whatever Sarah wanted.

"I'll follow you there to make sure that you don't make any detours," said Justin as he shut Sarah's door behind them. The three of them walked to Golish's office, no one saying a word.

"Identify yourselves," growled one of the sumo wrestler guards as the three of them reached Golish's office.

"It is I, Justin Bryant, escorting Sarah Setter who has an appointment with Mr. Golish, and Jack Clark who does not have an appointment but needs to see him due to his recent inappropriate behaviors."

"She may enter first," said one of the guards pointing a thick finger at Sarah, "because she has an appointment." The guards lowered their axes, and permitted Sarah to pass.

Justin leaned against the wall opposite the doorway while staring intently at Jack, as if inspecting him. Jack averted his gaze as he turned his back and began lightly drumming his fingers against the concrete wall, wanting to be back in Sarah's room, engaged in his first-ever kiss.

Several minutes later, Sarah emerged from Golish's office, her face streaked with tears. Before Jack could ask what was wrong, one of the sumo wrestler guards grabbed him by the shirt and dragged him into Golish's office with a single hand.

"Hey!" protested Jack, feeling abashed that he could be picked up by a single hand. The guards slammed the doors behind him, hiding Sarah from his view. Boiling with anger, Jack walked over to Golish's desk.

Golish looked worse than ever. His beard and hair were more rugged and untidy looking than Jack had ever seen. It looked as if Golish might fall asleep any second, his eyes seemed quite droopy. His desk was somehow even messier than the last time Jack had been in his office. A cigarette was pinched in-between two of Golish's fingers which explained why the office smelled horrible.

"Jack, take a seat," said Golish, coughing as he spoke. Jack tried to be polite, but he could not help wrinkling his nose. He had never been able to stand the smell of cigarettes. "I'm sorry," said Golish, "but I can't help it. It's pitiful, but I'm doing quite well now. I used to smoke marijuana, snort cocaine, and I was an alcoholic. I don't do those things very often now, although I haven't been able to quit smoking cigarettes." Jack cringed at the conversational way Golish spoke of drugs and alcohol. "But you're not here because of my drug problems. You're here because Justin caught you kissing Sarah in her room."

Jack's face turned red in embarrassment as Golish said this. He had never even kissed her in the first place. "Why does it matter? Justin hates me and is probably jealous that Sarah likes me." Jack realized he sounded selfish and stuck-up, that he was so great, and he alone deserved Sarah.

"Truthfully it doesn't matter to me. But Justin wanted you to come here, and I must do simple things that Justin wants."

"Why? You don't have to listen to Justin. You're the leader of Walkrins, not him!

"I agree. Justin is a miserable human being who spends his spare time spreading his misery to others. I don't like him anymore than you do. But he's invaluable for reasons I can't disclose, and therefore I must keep him happy. Don't let him get to you, just learn to ignore him. Please start spending less time with Sarah so Justin is not angered. "

"But I love her! I couldn't bear spend my evenings without her."

"Don't give me that love bullshit. Look, the best thing for everyone is to forget about any feelings you have for Sarah, finish your training with Rax, and then destroy the parasite. Understood?"

"Yes, sir," mumbled Jack.

"Excellent. You can leave now. Good day to you."

CHAPTER 25

Knowing that eating and sleeping were the most effective ways to alleviate frustration and anger, Jack headed down to the dining hall for dinner. A good meal and a nice long sleep was a pleasant prospect. Once in the dining hall, Jack spotted Fred and Rachel sitting together at one of the back tables, chuckling. He walked over to their table, feeling as if laughter and food were exactly what he needed.

"It was this massive, furry dog with these ridiculously large eyes," said Fred, waving his hands around animatedly. Rachel giggled hysterically, nearly falling off her chair at Fred's words.

"Hey guys," said Jack as he sat himself down at the table.

Rachel waved her right hand in greeting while she pressed her left hand against her mouth in an attempt to stifle her giggling. Fred nodded at Jack before glancing at his watch. "Rachel, we need to be on the roof in ten minutes," he said. Rachel stood up from her seat, her giggling beginning to subside. "Sorry, Jack," said Fred. "Rachel and I have to do guard duty. We'll catch up later."

"See you later," said Rachel as she flashed Jack with a smile.

Fred clapped Jack on the back and then he walked with Rachel out of the dining hall, and toward the stairwell. Once they disappeared from sight, Jack grabbed a few turkey sandwiches from the center of the table and munched on them as he sat alone. It seemed as if everything was in his grasp, kissing Sarah, being cheered up by Fred and Rachel. But someone or something had to ruin it, Justin barging in, Fred and Rachel having to do guard duty. Nothing seemed to be going as planned.

Once back in his room, Jack succumbed to sleep, hoping it would momentarily erase his troubles. However, it was not a peaceful sleep, for

Jack began to have one of those dreams that magicians had, the real ones that would affect his life. This dream was inside the Oval Office. President Jones, whose body was controlled by the parasite, sat behind the resolute desk. Sitting opposite from the desk was a man who Jack did not recognize. The man was tall, muscular, and skinny with a pencil thin mustache.

"Enough said about your travels, Dick," said President Jones. The man, Jack realized, was Dick Wilkinson, who worked for the parasite. "The time has come to unleash an assault upon Walkrins."

"Master, this is a drastic move, why have you decided to act now?"

"My spy reported that the mission to obtain food and medical supplies went well. They believe that the mission went so well that they have decreased security, thereby becoming overconfident. They will be weak and unprepared when our army arrives."

"Does that mean you will be accompanying the army there, Master?"

"Oh, I wish, Dick. But my mundane Presidential duties force me to be elsewhere. I have to go to a United Nations meeting; my plane takes off in a few hours. Instead, you will lead the army."

"What will the army be comprised of, Master?"

"Every surviving Treegont, which is about six hundred total. All of Tom's men which is around four hundred total. And the three Joinxs, of course. Our army will have over a thousand strong soldiers and Walkrins doesn't even have two hundred total members. We will easily crush them."

"How soon will the army be sent, and when should I arrive?"

"Tom and Lord Treegont began leading their troops up the mountain several days ago. I have a helicopter standing by that will take you to their current location. The pilot knows exactly where to take you. Once you arrive, you are to march straight to the hotel. Bring nothing but your sword. Do you understand?"

"Yes, Master." Dick hesitated. "Aren't you worried that the spy who has supplied you with information for years could be killed? Don't you want to spare the spy's life?"

"If they are all killed there will be no more need for the spy to give me information."

"And you still won't tell me who this spy is?"

"There's no need to tell you."

"Yes, Master," murmured Dick obediently. "I have one other question. What about my daughter?"

"She will be fine; she is more resourceful than you realize. Destroy Walkrins and all that Grassemer has fought for. Most importantly, bring glory to the all-powerful parasite who shall rule this world! Prepare the army, and begin the assault as soon as you can!"

Dick stood up, bowed to President Jones, and departed from the Oval Office, a determined expression upon his face.

CHAPTER 26

The dream ended, and Jack's eyes flew open. Without hesitation, he threw off his bedcovers, and departed from his room. Although he was still angry at how Golish had treated him, he knew that Golish had to be the first one to be notified of the oncoming assault. The hallways, which were dimly lit by candles, appeared to be completely empty. Jack did not know what time it was, but it did not matter, he had to tell Golish they were about to be attacked.

As Jack drew closer to Golish's office, both of the sumo wrestler guards came into view. They crossed their axes as Jack approached, their hulking forms towering over him.

"Who goes there?" asked the guard on the left.

"It is I, Jack Clark, here to see Mr. Golish."

Neither of the guards lowered their axes. They stared down at Jack, clutching their axes.

"I need to get inside," said Jack urgently.

"If you do not have an appointment, you cannot go inside," said the guard on the right.

"But we're about to attacked, I have to warn Golish!" shouted Jack. The guards made no reaction. "Golish! Golish!" shouted Jack, hoping the Walkrins' leader would hear him. "Golish!" The guards finally lowered their axes, but it was not to let Jack enter. They were pointing their weapons in Jack's direction, causing him to step backwards. "Golish!" bellowed Jack. At last, Golish thrust open the door, bleary-eyed and clad in pajamas.

"What's going on?" he asked in confusion.

"This boy is trying to get in without an appointment," said the guard on the right.

"But why?"

The guard faltered for a moment, and then said, "I'm not sure."

Golish gave an exasperated sigh. "I told you two that there were a few people you could let inside without appointments. Remember, Jack was one of them?" The guards stared blankly back at Golish, confused. "Oh, never mind. Now, Jack. What do you—?"

"I had a dream, one of those dreams that are real that magicians get. It was with the parasite and Dick Wilkinson. They're launching a full scale assault which could be here in less than an hour."

Golish looked at Jack, dumbfounded for a moment, the implications of Jack's words sinking in. As the horror of the situation dawned on him, a terrified expression overtook Golish's features. He glanced down at his hands as they curled into fists, and then back at Jack. "Come inside," he whispered, gesturing at Jack. Golish shut the door behind him as his guards resumed their usual positions. Golish walked behind his desk and slumped into his chair as Jack seated himself on the opposite side, just like their previous meetings. "Sorry about the guards," muttered Golish. "I saved them from being persecuted by a bookie who they wrestled for. They were so thankful that they offered to be my bodyguards. They're faithful, but not the brightest. But what do they matter compared to this full scale assault? Please, tell me everything about your dream."

Jack recounted every detail he could remember, from every word spoken to every little nuance. When he mentioned that the army would be over a thousand strong, Golish cried out in alarm, "A thousand strong! We don't even have two hundred total members, and some of them can't fight. How are we supposed to defeat them?"

Jack made no reply. He had no reason to believe that Walkrins could overcome the parasite's army.

The thought of impending doom hung in the air for a moment without Jack or Golish taking action. Then, Golish's hand dove into one of the many piles of paper on his desk. This time, his hand came out holding a black walkie-talkie. Golish punched a few buttons, and then held the device up to his lips. Seconds later, a familiar voice was crackling through the walkie-talkie.

"What's up, Golish?"

"Fred, I want you to abandon your post, and take the helicopter up into the sky. I've received a report that we're about to be attacked by an army of Treegonts and men working for Tom. Contact me once you're in the air, and tell me if you see the army. Circle around the area a few times before confirmation. And tell the other guards what's going on."

"Gotcha."

As soon as the sound of Fred's voice disappeared, Golish turned toward Jack. "Go back to your room, and get your father's sword. Then I want you to knock on everyone's door. Tell them it's an emergency and they need to go down to the marble entrance hall immediately. Warn everyone on the fourth, fifth, and sixth floor. I'll have Ryan warn everyone on the other floors. After you tell everyone, go straight to the library. Do you understand?"

Jack nodded, feeling for a moment as if his dream in the Oval Office was replaying. This time, Jack was Dick Wilkinson, sitting across from President Jones at his desk, giving orders, expecting Jack to come through. The whole situation felt wrong, Golish's formality and coldness, the idea that he could soon lose all his friends, even Sarah. Jack stood up from the chair, and walked out of Golish's office, past the spot where the spider had dangled when he had talked to Golish's several days ago, out of the doorway, past the sumo wrestler guards, and toward his room. Just as Golish ordered, Jack retrieved his father's sword from his room as he belted the weapon and its black sheath to his side. He took a quick glance around the pristine room before departing, hoping that it, along with the rest of the hotel and the people inside would remain intact despite the approaching assault. Then, Jack shut the door behind him, and began carrying out Golish's next instruction. He knocked on every door, telling each person exactly what Golish said. When there was no answer, Jack continued to rap his fist against the door, determined that no one would be forgotten. The first person he decided to notify was the person he cared about the most.

"Sarah, wake up!" yelled Jack as he pounded on her door. She came almost immediately, looking rather confused and bleary-eyed, but still beautiful.

"What is it, Jack?" she murmured sleepily as she brushed some of her silky black hair out of her eyes.

"There's an emergency. Alert as many others as you can and then head down to the marble entrance hall." Sarah nodded, still looking quite sleepy, and Jack proceeded to the door next to hers to tell as many others as possible about what was going on.

Gradually, everyone began spilling out of their rooms, confused and sleepy, most of them still clad in pajamas. The stairwell became clotted with people attempting to reach the first floor where the marble entrance hall resided. Even the elevator, which Jack had never seen being used before, was being used to transport crowds down to the entrance hall. He spotted Ricardo wheeling Juan in and taking his brother down.

Half an hour later, after he had notified everyone on the fourth, fifth, and sixth floors, Jack made his way down to the first floor. He struggled to move past the sluggish crowds, but he eventually made it down to the first floor, as he briskly walked toward his destination. The chestnut door to the library was flanked by both of the sumo wrestler bodyguards. This time, they merely nodded at Jack and allowed him to enter the library, hoping to find consolation in the place where his relationship with Sarah had grown, where he would find answers.

The first person Jack noticed upon entering was not Golish, but Robert Rax who stood in between two of the bookshelves, his shaved head bowed, his fingers curled around the hilt of his sword. Golish paced back and forth across the concrete floor, muttering under his breath as he glanced down at the walkie-talkie clutched in his hand. Rax inclined his head at Jack's entry, but Golish was oblivious as he continued to have a mumbled conversation with himself. The sight somehow gave Jack a slight comfort. This pacing, muttering Golish seemed more like the man Jack knew, not the formal leader barking orders.

"Golish, he's here," said Rax solemnly.

Golish snapped out of his mumbling and fixated his eyes on Jack.

"Everyone's in the marble entrance hall, just like you wanted," said Jack.

"Good work," said Golish, giving an approving nod. Jack was about to ask what to do next when a crackling noise emitted from the walkie-talkie. Relief flooded Golish's face at the sound. He pressed one of the buttons, and held the device unnecessarily close to his face, nearly touching his lips. "What do you have for me, Fred?" asked Golish, trying to keep his voice steady. There was no reply. "Hello?"

"This is Fred Waxston."

"I know. Now tell me, what do you see from the air? Do you see any army at all? If so, is it as big as the report indicated? How close are they to our base?"

"The reports were dead-on. They should be on sight in thirty minutes."

"Thirty minutes!" sputtered Golish. He nervously tugged at his beard. "Do you have anything else for me, Fred?"

"Yeah, I'm not coming back."

"What the hell are you talking about?"

"Rachel and I aren't coming back. We can't face him, and neither can you."

"What are you—?"

"I'm sorry, Golish. You're on your own."

"Now wait just a—"

The other side of the line went dead. Golish stared at the device, disbelief clouding his face, then replaced by despair.

CHAPTER 27

Golish sank to the concrete floor, gazing at the walkie-talkie as if it had been his last hope. Moans began escaping his lips, just like the time Jack had come to his office to discuss his father, and instead had had to listen to Golish complain. Again, Jack watched Golish's bizarre behavior, still not knowing how to help him. The worst part was that the man moaning on the floor was supposed to be a leader, one who could rally and unite people in a time of crisis.

Luckily, Rax was not as perplexed as Jack. "Get up, Golish," he barked in a voice filled with more emotion than Jack had ever heard. Golish continued to moan and clutch the walkie-talkie, but he did not rise up from the floor. He looked like a child refusing to do what his father wanted. "I said, get up!" snarled Rax. Golish made no movement. Frustrated, Rax strode forward, and began shaking Golish by the shoulders. "Goddamn, Golish, you're supposed to be the leader of Walkrins. Grassemer and the other founders are dead. You're the only one left, the only person the people will trust." Golish slowly lifted his head, his fearful eyes staring into Rax's face.

"We should retreat into the tunnel."

"What good would that do? We have to make a stand, and you need to be the one who rallies the troops."

"I can't do it, Rax. I was always the weakest founder."

"But you can't let them know that. They have faith in you."

Golish shook his head. "I'm sorry, I can't speak to them, but I can stand there if you want."

"Is that the best you can do?" Golish gave an embarrassed nod. Rax responded with a harsh laugh. "Well, I suppose that'll have to do. I guess

I'll do all the talking. We're going up to the second floor, where I'll address the entire organization. Golish, I want you on my left side, Jack, be on the right. Neither of you need to say anything, just stand there. They'll want to see their leader and hero before battle." Rax pulled Golish off the floor, clapped him on the back, and began walking out of the library. Golish followed, hanging his head like an ashamed child. Jack trailed behind the two men and the sumo wrestler guards as the chestnut door was closed and they headed up to the second floor.

Jack walked in a daze, unable to accept the current predicament. His new home, his peers, his friends, his life, could potentially be obliterated by the oncoming army. Worse yet, Fred and Rachel, the couple that welcomed him to Walkrins with open arms, accepting him immediately, were gone.

"Rachel and I aren't coming back. We can't face him, and neither can you."

The words echoed in Jack's mind, confusing and disturbing him. It was their abandonment that he found disturbing, that in the end their apparent loyalty was for naught. What confused him was the individual Fred claimed that he and Rachel couldn't face, and neither could Golish. For Jack, it was not one individual that frightened him, but the entire army. The idea of six hundred Treegonts converging on him, tearing his flesh apart, his bodily shell devoured until he ceased to exist. And it could happen in less than a second.

"Keep your eyes on the people, not me," muttered Rax as they began climbing up the stairwell, bringing Jack out of his morbid thoughts. "Give them the impression that we have the situation under control and that you're there for them. Guards, don't block Golish, I want him in plain view. And Golish, pick up your head." Rax halted as he came to the door. He looked at it for a moment, his body still, most likely gathering his thoughts before he addressed Walkrins. Then, he pushed open the door, and strode onto the second floor, over to the black iron railing.

Shouts came up from the crowd below as Rax, Jack, Golish, and the sumo wrestler guards came in sight. Below, the marble entrance hall was crowded, but not packed to the maximum thanks to the large size of the hall.

"Silence!" bellowed Rax. He waited until the shouting ceased before continuing. "We've received a report that an army of six hundred Treegonts and four hundred men has been sent to destroy us." The shouting from the crowd resumed, panic now mixed with confusion. "Silence!" bellowed Rax, again. "It's been confirmed by one of our own members that the report is accurate. The army will be on sight in less than thirty minutes." Rax did not mention that the member who confirmed this fact had fled. "Now don't worry, we've formed a plan for this type of scenario. We split into three units. Two of them will be located on the ground, and one will be on the hotel roof. The unit on the roof will be comprised of twenty snipers, led by Justin. One of the ground units will be led by me, the other one by Golish. Each ground unit will hide behind the horizontal boulders.

"The enemy army, which we expect to march directly to the hotel, will appear to have a free path. When the first line of the army passes the boulders, the ground groups will jump out and attack. Hopefully, the ground troops will heavily deplete the enemy's forces. Unless by some miracle the ground troops obliterate the entire enemy army, the snipers will fire once our enemies reach the empty expanse of grass in front of the hotel. Our goal is to destroy their army and prevent them from reaching the hotel. Before I tell you all what group you're part of I need to know if there are any questions." Rax paused, his eyes darting around the marble entrance hall, looking for a confused soul.

No one spoke, no one raised objections. The members of Walkrins were now stricken with fear, not confusion. They understood the doom that awaited them. In this moment of fear, they gazed up at Rax, the man who seemed to have the answers, who would deliver them from crisis.

Seeing that there were no questions, Rax plowed on. Somehow, he had memorized who was part of each unit, and began shouting down to each person, telling them which unit they were part of. They were to retrieve weapons from their rooms and then report to their leaders, either on the ground or on the roof. Jack listened as those he knew were assigned to their units: Sarah and Ricardo were with Golish, Ryan was with Rax, and Tony was with Justin. The only people who didn't seem to be part of a unit were Juan and Jack.

"You're going to be in the camera room with Juan," said Rax, as he finished shouting the last name, walking over to Jack.

"Why can't I fight?"

"Because we can't afford to lose you. We need you to destroy the parasite. But it's not coming. Only its army is."

"But after all my training, after everything I've been through I—"

"Rax is right, Jack."

Jack wheeled around at the sound of Sarah's voice, at first happy to see her, then angry that she was not siding with him.

"Rax is right," repeated Sarah in a soft, but much more solemn voice than usual. Jack looked into her attractive, flawless face, trying to read her thoughts. She knew he was not destined to destroy the parasite, so why didn't she want him to fight?

She wants to protect me, realized Jack, honored by her love, but embarrassed that she was the one protecting him, and not vice versa. For Rax and Sarah, the battle was won. Jack could not deny Sarah's wishes.

"Understand that you're not just being put there for protection," said Rax. "If the enemy army breaches the hotel, you'll be our last hope. Also, you can see how the battle is progressing." Rax hesitated. "I want you to know that it's been an honor training you, Jack." Rax stuck out his hand. Jack eyed it for a moment, his mind reeling back to the moment when they first met in the Fighting Complex, before he knew Rax, or almost anyone from Walkrins. The man who had at one time been nothing more than a solemn swordsman, was now a symbol of hope, the true hero that Jack believed Walkrins needed. Jack grasped Rax's hand, and looked into his deep gray eyes. Then, Rax strode across the second floor balcony, and disappeared down the stairs, closely followed by Golish and the sumo wrestler guards.

As Jack turned around, he found himself face to face with Sarah. She opened her mouth as if to speak, but instead of saying anything she flung her arms around Jack, hugging him tightly. "I had to agree with Rax," she whispered. "I couldn't risk losing you. *We* can't risk losing you."

"But you know I'm not destined to destroy the parasite," he muttered.

"You know how much I love you, Jack. If you were to die…" She trailed off, her arms tightening around Jack.

"Listen, if it looks bad, just run away," said Jack before he could help himself.

"And you stay in the camera room no matter what you see," she whispered back.

"I will."

They stood together for a moment longer, their arms wrapped tightly around each other. Then, Jack felt Sarah pulling away from him, her smooth skin brushing against him as she whispered, "Goodbye, love." He opened his eyes and watched her walk down the hallway, praying that he would be reunited with her after the battle.

"Aren't ya supposed to be in the camera room?"

Jack turned around at the sound of the voice. Standing behind him was Tony, a machine gun slung over his shoulder, wearing his eye patch, looking confused. "Oh yeah," said Jack, beginning to walk down the hallway.

"You take care of yourself, Jack," said Tony, eying Jack with his remaining eye.

"You do the same," said Jack. "Make sure you shoot all the Treegonts so I don't have to deal with them."

Tony grinned. "I'll do my best." They walked together, in silence, up the stairwell. When they reached the sixth floor, Tony walked over to a ladder hanging from the ceiling. "Up to the roof," he said, jerking his thumb upwards. "So, I guess I'll see ya soon," said Tony as he began climbing up the ladder. Once he disappeared from sight, Jack walked further down the hall, toward Juan.

"This is the camera room," said Juan, pointing to the door his wheelchair was situated in front of. With a grunt, he pushed the door open, waited for Jack to walk through, and then began wheeling himself inside.

The room was covered in rows of camera screens, showing what was happening both inside the hotel, and outside. Judging by the number of screens, Fred had been telling the truth when he told Jack that Walkrins was loaded with cameras. Then, Jack realized Fred was no longer in the vicinity, he had fled with Rachel. He wondered if anyone had even noticed their absence.

It doesn't matter, we can win this battle without them, thought Jack, trying to convince himself that Fred and Rachel's absence would cause no harm.

He turned his thoughts away from them and back to the camera screens. Inside, the screens showed every hallway, the stairwell, the elevator, the marble entrance hall, the kitchen, the dining hall, the library, the Fighting Complex, the basketball court, the exercise room, and storage rooms. Outside, the cameras showed the hotel, the wide expanse of grass, the boulders, many of the trees, and a good portion of nearby ground. It seemed that the only places there weren't cameras were in individual rooms and the dandelion meadow. Jack seated himself in the middle of one of the camera rows, trying to absorb what he saw. He repeatedly swiveled around in his chair, attempting to look at each screen. Juan wheeled himself beside Jack, eying the screens. The inside of the hotel appeared devoid of human presence. Cameras that Jack assumed were fixed to the trees showed the snipers arranging themselves on the roof, lying down on their stomachs, looking to Justin for orders.

On the ground, Golish and Rax attempted to organize their groups, having them hide behind trees, boulders, and bushes. Some of those with guns were climbing up trees. Rax seemed to have control over his unit which he was successfully organizing. Golish, on the other hand, was having a much more difficult time. The sumo wrestler guards followed him whenever he moved, sometimes shielding him from sight. Jack watched as he attempted to ward them off, trying to explain to them that he was in no danger at the moment. If not for the terror of their current situation, Jack suspected he would have found the scene quite amusing.

Eventually, Golish and Rax fully organized their units with everyone somewhat hidden or camouflaged. Then, they waited, the seconds dragging on as the sun rose.

"I wish I was fighting alongside my brother," said Juan unexpectedly, breaking the silence.

"I wish I was fighting alongside Sarah," said Jack without taking his eyes off the camera screen which showed Sarah hiding behind an oak tree. "But we have our orders."

"Screw orders, I would go down if it wasn't for this goddamn wheelchair," said Juan self-pityingly.

"We still might get a chance to fight," said Jack. "We're the only hope if the parasite's army gets into the hotel."

"I wouldn't be able to do much good. All I have is a pistol. If they get in here, you're on your own, kid."

Jack made no response. Silence resumed between them. They watched for ten minutes, a half hour, and then an hour, until the sun was fully risen. Jack was beginning to hope that his dream had been a delusion; no army was coming to destroy Walkrins. But as soon as this thought crossed his mind, the army materialized onto the screens.

Interspersed with each other, hundreds of Treegonts and ragged men marched side by side. Exhaustion was visible in the men's rugged faces, the slow movements of their bodies beneath their tattered clothes. Most of them had machine guns slung over their shoulders, and Jack knew that despite the long march up the mountain, none of them would show mercy, none of them would hesitate to kill. They were too well trained and brainwashed by Tom.

The Treegonts, however, appeared unaffected by the journey up the mountain. Their slimy bodies moved with an unmistakable sense of force, their pointed yellow teeth bared, a blur of dark green movement. Many of them clutched spiked metal rods, just like Jack had seen in the forest behind his school. Others carried long, wooden spears and bows and arrows which were slung over their backs.

The army marched in straight lines, except for the one individual leading the procession. The individual was not as Jack would have expected, Dick or Tom. The leader was not even human. A lone Treegont led the army, a thick beard of yellow leaves visible on his chin, his green slime not as dark as his brethren. But the most noticeable thing about the Treegont was the spear he held high above his head, and the object perched on the point of the spear. Jack stared at the camera screen, unable to make out the object.

Then, with a dawning sense of horror and disgust, he realized what it was: Grassemer's head.

Jack had not seen Grassemer killed, so he did not know how Tom committed the final murder, but he had never imagined that it had been decapitation. A wave of fury rolled over Jack, and he suddenly found himself grasping the hilt of his father's sword, determined to slay those responsible for Grassemer's death.

As the enemy army continued to march forward, following the Treegont who held Grassemer's head high in the air, Jack noticed one of the snipers beginning to move on the roof. It was Justin, who appeared to be aiming his sniper rifle at the Treegont. Before anyone knew what was happening, Justin was firing at the Treegont. Orange blood spouted from the Treegont's body as bullets pierced its slimy skin, the wooden spear falling out of its hands. For a moment, Grassemer's head was seen flying through the air. As it thudded to the ground, the enemy army split into two groups and charged at the ground units.

The battle had begun.

CHAPTER 28

Members of Walkrins emerged from behind boulders, bushes, and trees as the parasite's army charged at them, drawing their weapons, starting a charge of their own. Those with guns began firing at the opposition. Jack watched as soldiers from both sides went from charging the enemy, to crumpling to the ground, bullet-riddled, clutching bleeding wounds. Chaos escalated as the two armies clashed with one another, creating a sea of struggling bodies. The Treegonts brandished their long, metal, spiked rods, screaming at the top of their lungs as they hacked members of Walkrins to pieces. Orange blood flowed as their green flesh was torn apart by bullets and sword blades.

Apart from the Treegonts, Jack could no longer tell who was on which side. All he saw were humans killing one another as the ground became littered with bloody corpses. He couldn't even tell if anyone close to him, anyone he cared about was dead or alive. The only people he was able to recognize were Golish's two sumo wrestler guards, swinging their axes with muscular arms, eliminating all who stood in their path. It didn't look like they were even conscious of whether the humans were part of Walkrins, or if they worked for Tom.

Suddenly, about ten Treegonts jumped onto both of the sumo wrestler guards' backs, pulling them down to the ground as they ripped their skin apart with spiked metal rods. The next moment, the sumo wrestler guards were out of sight, among the other corpses, trampled by those still fighting.

Jack continued to watch the battle, unable to turn away, yet horrified by the sickening randomness of the killings. It did not matter who anyone was or what they had done. All that mattered was that they were an enemy who had to be killed. Regardless of positioning, no one was safe. The survivors were not necessarily any better than the dead, they were just luckier. Once the fighting started, logic was often ineffective.

Jack's eyes darted to each screen, searching for those he cared about, while it took all his willpower to stay rooted to his seat. If only he could help them… But Sarah had told him to stay in the camera room no matter what he saw. What did it matter? Everything seemed meaningless while watching senseless destruction. Sarah could already be dead. The Walkrins' army was heavily depleted. There was a chance they were all dead.

This thought was dismissed, but likely to become reality as Jack watched a throng of a mere thirty Walkrins' members break away from the battle, fleeing back toward the hotel. He identified Rax on the screen, bellowing orders, most likely for a retreat as he slashed Treegonts, who fell one by one as they met Rax's sword. The survivors sprinted across the expanse of grass, pursued by the parasite's army, which was largely intact. The snipers on the hotel roof began firing at the enemy army as they appeared. Tom's men and the Treegonts collapsed onto the grassy expanse as the snipers fired down on them, bloodied and mutilated.

But it was not enough. The Treegonts were firing back with their bows and arrows, and Tom's men with their machine guns. Snipers fell off the roof, plummeting to the ground as the Treegonts' arrows buried into their chests and bullets tore their flesh apart.

Suddenly, Jack caught sight of a familiar face dashing toward the hotel: Golish. His bodyguards were dead, but he had survived. Treegonts began closing in on him, but he was saved as Justin hit them with clean headshots. It looked like he was about to make it back with the other survivors until Jack noticed a cloaked figure sprinting toward him. As the figure came closer, the hood fell back, revealing the blank face of a blonde-haired man.

It was Fred Waxston.

But as Jack looked closer, he saw that the face was too aged to be Fred's, too devoid of emotion. It could only be one person: Ben Waxston, the third Joinx.

As Golish turned around, Ben pounced on his old friend, thrusting a sword through his throat. For a split second, Golish looked into his friend's vacant face, and then his head drooped backwards, blood pooling from his throat.

Just when Jack thought he had seen the worst of the battle, a Treegont launched an arrow up toward the roof, sending it straight through Tony's skull.

Jack diverted his eyes from the screen before he could see Tony's body plummet to the ground, or the blood spurting out of his pierced skull. He stood up from his seat, and began walking out of the camera room, filled with simmering anger.

"We're not supposed to leave the camera room until the hotel is breached or the battle is over," said Juan, swiveling around in his wheelchair.

"Screw orders," said Jack, echoing Juan's earlier words. He pushed open the door to the camera room, not hesitating to see if Juan was going to follow him. Once out of the camera room and on the sixth floor, Jack walked over to the black railing, peering over it, down into the marble entrance hall.

The survivors were crammed into the small space in front of the metal doors leading into the hotel, attempting to ward off the oncoming attack. Slowly, they were being forced back farther and farther, their numbers dwindling as bloodied bodies keeled over, overwhelmed by weaponry and sheer numbers.

Suddenly, five men burst through the defenders, machine guns in hand. One of them glanced up and saw Jack. He aimed his weapon up at the sixth floor, firing a series of bullets. As Jack flung himself onto the concrete floor in order to avoid the bullets, Juan wheeled himself in front of Jack, all the bullets burying themselves in the handicapped man's chest. For a second, Jack saw Juan's lifeless, bloodied body slump into his wheelchair, his head hanging like a limp ragdoll. Then, Jack's own blood began trickling down his forehead, slowly running down his face as he passed out.

CHAPTER 29

"Is he dead?"

"What do you think, Albert?" said an unfamiliar voice in a mocking tone. "He's not breathing, he's not moving, and his forehead's bleeding like mad. Sometimes I think you should just go back to begging on the streets. You're the dumbest piece of shit I've ever met."

Before the man called Albert could make a retort, Jack heard another unfamiliar voice, this one much more authoritative.

"The battle is far from over. There are still survivors. Go back down, finish them off, and dispose of this Mexican's body. I will attend to the boy, whether he is dead or alive," said the voice.

"Yes, Tom," murmured the one called Albert.

Several seconds passed as the sound of the men's footsteps faded down the hallway, accompanied by Juan's wheelchair creaking against the concrete floor as his corpse was pushed away. Then, Jack felt a large, meaty hand upon his pulse. The hand's touch was quickly released, replaced by the sensation of powerful arms picking Jack off the concrete floor. Jack felt himself being gently placed into a chair, the same kind of chair that was in the camera room. As Jack heard a door being shut, he opened his eyes, curious to see his rescuer. His heart nearly stopped at the sight of the portly man with the bald head and bushy mustache standing across from him, his right hand resting on the pommel of his sword.

"Thank goodness you're alive, Jack," said Tom softly. He grew still, his eyes fixated on Jack's face.

"Why do you care that I'm alive?" asked Jack furiously. "Were you worried that someone else would kill me, worried that you wouldn't be able to prance back to your Master and present my head to him? Or is it

165

unfinished business, you want to kill both the father and son?" Tom's reply would not matter; Jack was only trying to distract him so he could attack his father's killer at the opportune moment.

"Please hear me out, Jack. I do not want to kill you," said Tom in a trembling voice. Jack made no response, he was sure that the parasite's servant was trying to deceive him. "We are not so different, you and I," continued Tom whose voice was now somewhat steadier. "Before anyone realized our true talents we were bullied as if we were rotten scum. We both had very few people who cared about us, or who we cared about. I had my friends Dick and Durog, as well as my father. You had your mother." He paused, and took a step closer to Jack. "Eventually, our true abilities were recognized, and those who were striving for dominance and power seized us. We were powerful tools for them. I was recruited by the parasite who wanted to control the world, you were recruited by Grassemer who wanted to do the same, although I'm sure he did not tell you this."

This was the time to strike at Tom, yet Jack remained still.

"The parasite and Grassemer blinded us with visions of making the world a better place. They claimed that we would be quite instrumental in the process. The parasite convinced me that I would be making the world a better place by eliminating the flaws of humanity. Grassemer told you that you would be making the world a better place by fighting *his* enemies who you should have no concern about, except for me because I killed your father. Of those that you fight I am the only one who you should be fighting. The parasite, Dick, and the others did nothing to harm you before you were recruited by Grassemer."

Jack could not understand why Tom was telling him these things. He was now somewhat interested in what Tom was saying, part of him wanted to hear more, part of him wanted to slay this man who had killed both his father and mentor.

"Both of our fathers were also killed by power-hungry fools. Yes, Jack, I am calling myself a power-hungry fool; I have been one ever since I started serving the parasite. Grassemer killed my father during the magicians' war, and as you know, I killed your father. You may not believe me, but I do feel remorse for murdering him. He was not a bad man. He was merely blinded by Grassemer. It was wrong of me to kill him. But I feel no remorse for killing Grassemer. He was a vile man who was no better than the parasite. He may have appeared to be a good man who had your best interests at heart, but he truly only pretended to be kind so his power-hungry schemes could prevail."

Jack continued to sit motionless in the chair, his forehead caked in blood, his heart thumping. He was waiting to strike at Tom; he figured the reason why Tom had told him all this was near. After that, he would attack Tom, and avenge the death of his father.

"There is no good and evil in this war. There are only two sides who want to gain power," said Tom as he took a step closer to Jack. "For too long I have blindly followed the parasite. You have also followed blindly, except you have followed Grassemer and Walkrins. Join me, Jack. Together, with our strength, we can end this pointless war. The first thing we will do is make sure your mother is safe and have her join our cause. I will personally ensure that your family no longer suffers. Four hundred men are under my command, their allegiance lies with me. Together we will end this war and bring peace to the world!"

As Tom finished speaking, Jack ripped his sword out of its sheath. The sword that had once been Jason Clark's was clenched in Jack's hand, ready to kill the man who had killed its original owner. Jack grasped the monkey engraved hilt, leapt up from the chair, and stabbed Tom right in the heart. Terror flooded Tom's face as blood oozed from his body. He made no attempt to attack Jack. Whether this was because he could not or he had been telling the truth, Jack would never know. Feeling he had done enough damage, Jack heaved his sword out of Tom's heart. As soon as Jack pulled out his sword, Tom thudded to the floor, his eyes staring blankly ahead, blood seeping out of his body.

Jack had thought he would feel satisfied, maybe even elated after killing Tom, as he avenged his father's death. He had foolishly believed that killing Tom would amend his father's death, as if it would fill the void of a fatherly figure Jack had always yearned for. Jack had expected to feel courageous and triumphant after killing Tom. He could not identify what emotions he was feeling, except he knew they were all negative. He shook as he stared down at Tom's lifeless body.

I'm a monster, thought Jack bitterly. *Tom spared my life, he was offering to help me and what did I do? A single thrust of my sword and his whole life, everything he ever worked for was snuffed out in an instant.*

Tom's life work may have been amoral for the most part, but had he not just revealed a desire to seek redemption? A desire to relinquish the grip of the sword and embark on the quest for peace. But any chance for redemption, self-improvement, and goodness were destroyed when Tom's life ended.

Jack turned his gaze away from Tom's corpse and looked down at the bloody sword which had once been his father's. He had initially viewed the object as almost sacred, for it was his only keepsake that had been his father's. Now he felt repulsed by it, its once shiny blade soaked in scarlet blood, still dripping onto the floor.

Unable to look at Tom's corpse any longer, Jack's eyes drifted toward the camera screens, only to see more death and destruction. It was even worse than last time. Bloodied corpses were strewn across the marble entrance hall, staining the once flawless floor. Body parts were scattered, mutilated arms, legs, and parts that were beyond identification. On another screen, an unrecognizable, bloody figure was stumbling across the first floor hallway. Thinking that maybe it was Sarah or someone else he cared for, Jack stuck his bloodied sword back in its sheath, stepped over Tom's lifeless body, and began sprinting down to the first floor.

Less than a minute later, he emerged into the dining hall as he spotted the bloody figure teetering in between tables. The figure raised its head at the sound of approaching footsteps.

"Jack."

There was something familiar in the tone of that voice, softness, once prominent, now mixed with a somewhat raspy tone. Realizing who it was, Jack ran forward and caught the wobbly figure of Ryan Longring before he hit the ground. Ryan twitched on the floor, his hands clawing at his charred face, his shirt soaked in blood. Jack had only been able to identify Ryan because of his distinct tone of voice, but even that unique quality seemed marred by battle.

"What happened?" shrieked Jack, angered and frightened over his friend's current predicament.

"Explosion," croaked Ryan.

"What do you mean?"

"One of our own, someone from Walkrins threw an explosive. I think they were throwing it at an enemy group that breached the hotel, but I can't be sure. I happened to be nearby and…" Ryan trailed off as he rolled onto his side and began howling. Ryan Longring, a kind, intelligent, and dignified man was now a crying, grotesque disfigurement. No cataclysmic event had occurred to spark such a radical transformation. Ryan had simply been in the wrong place at the wrong time.

"You're a doctor, Ryan, you must know how to help yourself!" cried Jack frantically. "Just tell me what to do and I'll be able to help you."

Ryan did not respond, but continued to roll around on the floor in excruciating pain. Thinking that maybe Ryan could be saved if the bleeding was stalled, Jack turned his back on his friend and began scouring the dining hall, searching for something that would do the job.

"Ryan, what's best to use when you want to stop someone from bleeding?" asked Jack with his back still turned.

Ryan gave no reply. In fact, he was no longer screaming. Jack wheeled around, curious to find the reason for Ryan's sudden silence. Ryan was now standing a few feet away from Jack, his burnt face contorted in pain, a sword protruding from his stomach.

Holding that sword, her face as impeccable as ever, was Sarah.

"The faggot doesn't seem to have much to say," said Sarah maliciously as she yanked the sword from Ryan's stomach.

"What's going on, Sarah?" asked Jack who felt more frightened than he had during the whole battle.

"I don't think your puny brain could handle the information," said Sarah as she wiped Ryan's blood off her sword and onto a nearby table.

"Why did you murder him?" screamed Jack, a note of hysteria in his voice. Footsteps echoed from the first floor hallway as Jack spoke. Treegonts arrived at the scene, their bows and arrows pointed at Jack as they formed a circle around him and Sarah.

"Hold your fire and keep your positions," ordered Sarah to the Treegonts in a commanding voice. Jack did not understand; what authority did Sarah have over these Treegonts? Sarah leered down at Jack with much dislike, something he was not used to seeing from her. "You really are quite annoying," said Sarah as she finished wiping the blood off her sword. "I never liked you at all, Jack. I mean, you're hideously ugly, and not exactly the sharpest tool in the shed." She gave Jack a wicked grin as she continued speaking. "Oh you so believed I loved you as much as you loved me. I deceived you because I'm so good at acting; I always got the lead roles in my high school plays." Jack could hear a note of pride in Sarah's voice as she praised her own acting abilities.

"And why did you have to act, and pretend to like me?" asked Jack, who was gradually feeling more depressed than he had ever been in his life.

"Because my Master told me to," whispered Sarah in a dangerously quiet voice.

"And who's your Master?" asked Jack, although he already had an idea of the answer.

"How stupid can you get?" cried Sarah in a skeptical tone. "If I'm not on your side, of course I serve the parasite, you idiot!" She let out a maniacal laugh. "Oh you were so easily deceived by me; you thought I was the most wonderful thing in the whole world. Although I admit, sometimes it was tough pretending to like you when I had to look at your ugly face. The nausea people must feel when looking at you, you're so gross! You made my job easy by convincing yourself that I had fallen in love with you, just because you thought I was hot and we spent our evenings together. You spilled out your most dire secrets and practically your heart to me. You gave me a great deal of useful information that I relayed to my Master. Sometimes you told me too many pitiful details about your pitiful life that I didn't care to know."

Every harsh comment made Jack feel as if he was losing part of his heart, as if he was losing reasons to live. "Why did the parasite want to know these things about me?" asked Jack angrily.

"Yet again you display that your stupidity has no boundaries," said Sarah, shaking her head in an exasperated sort of way. "It's because the parasite thought you were the only threat, that you were the only one who could destroy it. My Master wanted to know everything about you, anything it could so it would discover your weaknesses and be able to destroy you. There were many times when I found myself quite skeptical that you truly were the only one who could defeat the parasite. Last night I found my skepticism turned out to be prophetic." She took a deep breath and began speaking in a mocking tone. "As you expressed your *feelings* for me, as if you actually believed that I loved you."

She began speaking in a normal voice again, but not before letting out a loud cackle of mad laughter that did not seem to belong to the Sarah Jack had known. "Your stupidity helped me through all this. You told me about that dream you had of me. If your mother hadn't woken you, everything could have been ruined. How could you possibly believe that I escaped from the three Joinxs at the Lincoln Memorial? They dragged me to the White House as their prisoner."

"If they captured you, why are you working for them?" asked Jack.

"All this time, you've told me about your past, but you never asked about mine. How foolish it was of you to think you love me when you are so self-centered. As if you could understand the concept of true love."

"I asked Golish about your past so I never thought there was any reason to talk about it!" retorted Jack angrily.

"Did you honestly believe that liar? He probably told you how my adoptive parents had fatal heart attacks, and you probably swallowed the ludicrous lie, just like me. Like me, you were too ignorant to realize the truth, the truth I discovered when I was imprisoned at the White House. They were executed by Golish because they were no longer fit for fighting. Can you believe it? I realized in that instant that Walkrins is no better than the parasite and its allies. Both sides are corrupt."

"If you believe the parasite is so horrible then why do you serve it?"

After Jack asked his question, a small stone flew out of Sarah's right hand. She caught it with the same hand as it came out, and began tossing it up and down.

"You can do magic?" asked Jack who couldn't believe Sarah had hid this ability along with her myriad of other lies.

"Oh what a genius you are," murmured Sarah. "Yes, it's been quite useful in my work. Now getting back to your original question, I serve the parasite for a reason that I don't think your puny brain could handle, so I won't waste my breath."

"You're wasting your life, so why not waste your breath?"

He felt like he was back at school with Trent bullying him. He had thought he had escaped that forever, but he should have known better. There were plenty of others like Trent who relished in the pain and sufferings of others. He didn't care what happened next, all he knew was that he would not let Sarah, or anyone else take advantage of him anymore.

Sarah's smile vanished as her eyes narrowed and her lips curled into a snarl. She walked toward Jack, her sword pointed at his chest. She spoke in a dangerous whisper. "I serve the parasite because it is the only way to keep my family intact. My father is Dick Wilkinson. My mother was a supermodel who he fell in love with for the wrong reasons. She took me away from my father soon after I was born. She was a selfish woman who did not genuinely care about people. She despised children, thought they were the most horrible things in the world. All she cared about was her modeling, and the number of men she had sex with each night. She ran away from my father, and dumped me by chance on the highway by this mountain. Neither side in this war is right. But if I have to fight on one side, I will fight for the side that gives the best chance of keeping me reunited with my father. You don't understand, but nothing is more important than family."

Her face was now inches from Jack's face. The tip of her sword was touching his Adam's apple. "I was supposed to kill you, but when I told the parasite that you are truly not the one who will destroy it, I was given new orders: to capture you so you will serve the parasite. The parasite could use your magical powers, despite how weak you are."

"I'd rather die than serve that monster," said Jack, trying to sound braver than he felt.

"You won't have a choice," she whispered menacingly. Jack waited for something to happen, but nothing did. Sarah stopped speaking, her sword still touching his Adam's apple. The Treegonts continued to surround Jack and Sarah, their bows and arrows still pointed at him.

There was dead silence until one of the Treegonts gasped and dropped its bow and arrows to the floor. As they all turned around to look at the Treegont, Jack saw a sword being withdrawn from its back by none other than Robert Rax. The Treegonts directed their bows and arrows at Rax, but before they could shoot, lava was shot at them from an unseen figure.

Treegonts crumpled to the floor and cried out in pain as Rax slashed and hacked at them, and the unseen figure that Jack now identified as Justin continued to pelt lava at them, searing their flesh. Sarah held her position, holding the sword at Jack's throat, but was forced to flee as Justin and Rax ran forward to attack her. She scampered out of the dining hall and up the stairwell, attempting to escape Justin's lava and Rax's sword, leaving Jack where moments before he had been held captive.

"Come on, follow me, we have to get out of here," said Justin. Without hesitation, Jack began following Rax and Justin.

"The hotel entrance is blocked," said Rax in an emotionless voice, "how are we supposed to get out?"

"We'll use the Emergency Exit," said Justin, pointing to the door and the bright red sign at the end of the dining hall.

"There aren't any other survivors?" asked Jack.

"I'm afraid not," said Justin solemnly, "but at least you survived." Jack did not understand it; Justin had always been so mean to him.

As Justin pushed open the Emergency Exit door, revealing an entrance to a dark tunnel, Jack asked, "Who are you?"

Rax disappeared into the tunnel. Before Justin followed him, he turned around, faced Jack, and said, "I am Justin Bryant, son of Grassemer Bryant."

CHAPTER 30

Dick Wilkinson stood on the wide expanse of grass in front of the hotel, surveying the carnage from the battle. A multitude of corpses littered the ground, the blood still fresh and oozing out of many of the bodies. There were the maimed, slimy Treegont corpses whose orange blood glistened on their bodies like bright rays of sun upon a field of grass. Then there were the human corpses, mangled and unrecognizable. Dick could not distinguish the members of Walkrins from Tom's men. It was merely a jumble of lifeless bodies, whose only purpose now was to rot and perhaps cause grief. Lying directly in front of Dick was a human corpse that hardly looked humane, the head had nearly been wrenched off the shoulders, and a jagged line of blood ran down its back, most likely pierced by a sword. Dick smiled as his foot pushed down on the dislodged head, causing further damage to the crushed skull.

This is the way things are supposed to be, survival of the fittest and strongest, thought Dick happily. *Humans think they are special and superior to all other creatures. The truth is that humans are nothing more than animals. The only difference is that humans questioned their existence and strove to discover purpose in their lives, which lead to their quest for domination. Animals on the other hand accepted the world as the way it was.*

Dick removed his foot from the mutilated head and perused the bodies for the corpse of a Treegont. When he identified one, he stooped over, peering at the bullet hole that pierced the Treegont's skull and snuffed out its life.

The world should be a battle among the strongest and fittest, life for all creatures should be a constant war, to ensure survival for themselves and those they love. It is this ideal and pure world that the parasite is determined to restore. We shall vanquish all the humans who destroyed that noblest manner of life. I was brainwashed to believe that the current way of life is just, but the parasite enlightened me, it revealed the truth. Animals we were, and animals we shall be!

Dick walked away from the Treegont corpse and returned to his thoughts, the nauseating stench of death filling his nostrils. No, it was not the stench of death. It was the scent of purity.

We should not wrestle with moral qualms, but rather do what is necessary to survive and protect our loved ones. That's how I convinced those soldiers to kill at the military base. Jessica and the others were a threat, so they had to be killed. Orders should be taken without question in the face of danger.

The three Joinxs passed in front of Dick, their faces concealed by the hoods of their cloaks.

I'm so glad that they captured Sarah, thought Dick. *If they hadn't, I may never have been reunited with her, my daughter that I love. However, the parasite saw her as far more than my daughter, but as a potential asset to our cause. She has gone above and beyond my expectations. Her ability to seduce Jack Clark and gather valuable information from him has been most helpful, especially this news that he has magical powers, yet is not destined to destroy my Master as Grassemer wanted us to believe...*

Dick reflected back on the journey up the mountain, how he had received the message from his daughter, the message that Jack was not truly destined to destroy their Master. After she told her father, Dick contacted the parasite, whose new orders were to capture Jack alive to be a new, powerful addition to their cause. The parasite chose Sarah for the assignment because of her ability to manipulate Jack. Dick only hoped that she had succeeded and that the Treegonts had obeyed her as instructed...

"Father!" cried Sarah.

Dick whirled around at the sound of her voice. His heart leapt at the sight of her, until he saw the tears pouring down her face, and that Jack was not with her. "Sarah, darling, what happened?" asked Dick concernedly as he ran forward to hug his sobbing daughter.

"I had him, father, I captured him, but..." She trailed off as she began to sob even more hysterically.

"But what, Sarah?" asked Dick impatiently, half eager and half frightened to learn the cause of his child's distress.

"Justin Bryant and Robert Rax attacked the Treegonts and escaped with Jack!"

Dick loosened his grasp on Sarah's shoulders and nearly collapsed onto the ground. No, his daughter must be lying, she could not have failed. Everything had been going so smoothly, all the cards were in their hands, yet Jack had escaped. Vengeance was a virtue for the parasite; it did not forgive easily. There was no doubt about it; there would be retribution against Sarah.

"Father, there's more bad news," said Sarah dejectedly.

More bad news, thought Dick, *there cannot be any more bad news, or any further blunders!*

"Tom is dead, I saw his body. He appears to have been stabbed."

This was too much for Dick. He fell to the ground, landing on a bloody, distorted Treegont corpse. Tom had been a friend of Dick's since childhood; he had been strong, powerful. No one could have defeated him. But if there was anything that Dick had learned over the years, it was that war was not theoretical.

"Father," murmured Sarah as she extended a hand.

Dick gazed up at his daughter who looked more unattractive than he could ever have imagined due to her blotchy, tear streaked face and miserable failure. There were many words that Dick wanted to say to her, but all he was able to utter was, "May the Almighty parasite have mercy on Tom's soul, on ours as well for our mistakes, and may it aid us in our quest to capture and wield Jack Clark."

END OF BOOK ONE